CLAWS
AND
FANGS

6

STAY
WITH ME

INTERNATIONAL BESTSELLING AUTHOR
SARAH SPADE

FOREWORD

Thank you for checking out *Stay With Me*!

This is a novella (~30,000 words) that brings the **Claws and Fangs** series to a close for now. I love this world, and I visit it in the **Stolen Mates** series, so I can't imagine leaving it for long. In fact, in 2023, I have a new Fang City to introduce you to, with a vamp hero and the human slayer that becomes his beloved, so I will definitely be writing more about supes!

With this book, though, I bring it full circle by featuring Trish Danvers and the Mountainside Pack. The "other female" from the first book, Trish went through a lot over the course of Gem and Ryker's story. By the end of *Forever Mates*, I knew I wanted to give her her own happily-ever-after. And no one is better for her than Duke, the gentle giant delta who has loved her from afar for years... she just didn't know it yet.

She doesn't when this novella begins, either—but she will, and I'm so glad that these two characters find their forever with each other. He's so good for her, and even though Trish might still be the selfish female who once schemed to come between Gem and Ryker, once she sets her sights on Duke, the big guy doesn't stand a chance.

I hope you enjoy!

xoxo,
Sarah

CHAPTER 1

NIGHTMARES

He's chasing me.

It's the same dream I've had for more than seven months now. I'm in my fur, dashing through a crowded woods, my ears flat against my skull, my white tail streaming behind me. As a she-wolf, I'm usually the predator; with the dark gold wolf dogging my every step, I'm the most enticing of prey. He snaps his jaws, almost closing on me before I swerve, barely avoiding his fangs.

There's laughter in his honey-gold eyes, a humor that is somehow also cruel and calculating. He has plans for me for when he finally runs me down. And while he uses his dominance against me, trying to get me to submit to his alpha nature, I'm so damn scared that my self-preservation wins out. I run because there's no alternative.

I can't let him catch me.

When I'm awake my human brain reminds me that this is nothing but a nightmare. In reality, Jack "Wicked Wolf" Walker never chased me, though the few times he lowered himself to gloat about taking me captive, the dark humor was written on his deceptively handsome face. If he decided to hunt me, I have no doubt it would play out just like it does in my dreams—but he didn't, because while I was prey, I wasn't his target.

I was his *bait*.

I also know that he can't chase me now anyway. The former Alpha of the Western Pack is dead, murdered by a pretty boy vampire who wanted to save his lone wolf mate from Walker's clutches.

Lucky her. When I was in a cage in the Wolf District, I knew no one was coming for me. I'd burned too many bridges with my Alpha and his mate to think they cared, and though I have friends and family among my packmates, I'm not the *one* to anybody. I don't have a mate, and I never thought a single soul would risk their hide for me.

But they did. Gemma—the female alpha of our pack, and the last shifter I expected to come to my rescue—took the trip from Accalia to the Wolf District, bringing two of her personal guards with her while Ryker, Mountainside's Alpha, stayed behind with the rest of the pack. And I know it wasn't just because I was trapped in a cage across the country from my home.

Gem was actually the Wicked Wolf's biological daughter, and she had her own score to settle with him.

She's not in my dreams. When her father chases me, it's just the two of us until my wolf collapses from exhaustion, Walker howling in triumph as he grips the scruff of my fur with his fangs, preparing to mount me.

That's how I know for sure it's not real. While shifters are part human, part beast, our human side rebels at the idea of mating while we're in our fur. It's just... it's not done. Even a sadistic bastard like Walker wouldn't try to mate me when I wasn't wearing my skin —which was exactly why I stayed in my fur nearly the entire time I was his prisoner.

Tonight's dream is different, though. Just when the ghost of Walker is stalking toward me, the air splits with a menacing growl of a bark. His ears twitch, one paw paused as he searches for the source of the sound, while I crawl a few paces away on my belly.

The wind whips by, the leaves over my head rustling. As the echo of the howl dies down, I don't hear anything else, which makes me wonder if I imagined it. Out of the corner of my eye, I see the dark gold wolf flick his ears again before padding forward. He's panting, but it's not because he just tore through the trees that surround his hidden territory in California.

He's panting because he's excited from the hunt, and I have no escape.

I whine, the sound pulling from my throat. In

response, another howl breaks through the night before thunderous paws pound against the ground. Seconds later, it becomes clear that they're heading straight for the clearing I collapsed in.

I find the strength to lift my head off of the dirt right as a moving shadow leaps out the darkness, landing beneath a stray moonbeam. The Luna bounces off of his sleek fur, flashing against his golden shifter's eyes.

It's a grey wolf, I see. Bigger than the Alpha, though his dominance is nowhere as strong, the grey wolf doesn't need to be a higher rank to get his point across. His size does it for him, as does the warning he puts into his rolling growl.

He's come for me—and he's not about to let Walker get in his way.

Instead of being frightened, I feel an inexplicable pull toward him. I don't know this wolf—at least, in my dreams, I don't—but there's something about him. He makes me feel safe, and if there's one thing I've craved more than having someone pick me for me, it's knowing that I'm protected.

The giant grey wolf... he'll protect me. It's just instinct. I have to get to him.

I yip. Too weak to do anything but move my muzzle, I gaze up at him. If I can get to him, everything will be okay. *I* will be okay.

If I just—

My eyes spring open. I'm laying on my naked belly, just like I was in my dream, only I'm in my two-legged, human form. Not surprising—I've maybe shifted a handful of times since I was rescued—but I'm completely bare in case I lose control while I'm asleep. I've sacrificed too many pairs of good pajamas to sleep-shifting, and it's my habit to strip down before climbing into bed.

Why not? It's not like I'm sharing it with anyone else...

Now that I'm awake, I give my head a clearing shake and shove my blanket away from my lower half. The thin covering is wrapped around my legs, another casualty of my recurring nightmare. I must've been "running" in my sleep and now my blanket is twisted all around me. Frustrated and still confused as to what woke me up so suddenly, I kick until I'm free.

Then—another habit—I take a deep breath, sampling the scents in the air.

It's the first week of May. Shifters of all types run hot, and though it's still chilly up on our mountaintop settlement this time of year, most of my packmates keep their windows open to the breeze. Not me. It would be easier to protect my territory—my cabin—if I could use my wolf's nose to scent any threats creeping up on me... but I can't. I need to know no one can sneak in through my window, even if it's harder to catch nearby scents through the glass windows and two wooden doors.

As a delta, my senses aren't as strong as other wolves, but I can still pick up the enticing aroma of bacon nearby regardless. That must be what woke me up. No self-respecting she-wolf can ignore the enticing scent of cooked meat when it's so close. Bacon especially is powerful enough to reach me inside of my sanctuary.

Climbing out of the bed, I pad over to my dresser. Nudity might not be a big deal to my kind of supe, but I already have a reputation in Accalia. For the most part, I've earned it. Doesn't mean that I'm going to prance around naked. The catty gossips—ironic since every Mountainside packmate is wolf—would love to have more ammunition to toss my way.

I can just hear them now.

Did you see the Danvers girl?

Still so desperate to attract a mate, she's walking around in her skin.

Make sure she doesn't set her eyes on your male because Luna knows that, if she made a play for the Alpha even after he had his intended, none of the rest of our mates are safe...

Because that's me. Trish Danvers, home-wrecker. Not even a home-wrecker, really. *Attempted* home-wrecker because, no matter how hard I tried to convince Ryker Wolfson that he should choose me over his fated mate, I never stood a chance.

I tried, though. Can't deny that. For most of my mature years—since I was about twenty and I decided my best chance at forever was with the future Alpha of the pack—I was fixated on making Ryker mine. It's all I wanted. The security of being the female alpha of the pack, and the protection of the most powerful wolf around. Plus, Ryker is gorgeous, and I honestly believed that I loved him.

Just like I believed that I would be a better mate for him than his own...

Since he was our Alpha's son, I always knew that I had until Henry passed and Ryker succeeded him to convince Ryker to choose me. It's how it's done. Alphas rarely take mates until they're installed as leader of the pack, and once they are, their Luna Ceremony follows closely on the heels of the one that makes them Alpha. I thought I had time—and then Henry died in an accident, and Ryker became Alpha when I was barely twenty-four.

And that's when all of Accalia discovered that the Luna whispered that his fated mate was the daughter of the Lakeview Pack's Alpha, an innocent-appearing omega who was only a year older than I was.

At first I thought I was doing them both a favor. A formidable alpha wolf, Ryker would've eaten an omega she-wolf alive. Especially blonde-haired, golden-eyed

Gemma, with her big smile and her bouncy curls. But then... Ryker never wanted me. Despite all of my efforts, I knew it. His attention was always elsewhere, and the first time I saw his dark gold eyes land on Gem when she wasn't watching, I knew.

She wasn't only his fated mate. She was his chosen mate. I'd lost him before I ever had him—and I was heartbroken.

Does that excuse what happened after? How I listened to our traitorous Beta's whispers when Shane Loup told me that Gem wasn't really an omega, but a rare alpha instead? Or how I blackmailed Ryker into choosing me otherwise I would tell the whole shifter world about her? Not to mention the countless ways I bullied our Alpha's intended, telling her that *I* was Ryker's chosen mate when he made it obvious time and time again that he only had eyes for her?

No. No, it doesn't. And while all of that happened two years ago, when I yank open the second drawer of my dresser and see the folded piles of sundresses packed inside, my stomach goes tight. I'd gone through a phase where I thought, if I styled my light brown hair in curls, and I pulled girly sundresses on that looked like Gem's when she was still passing as an omega, maybe Ryker would see what he was missing. It wasn't that unusual. A lot of she-wolves stick to simple dresses because they're easy to remove when we're getting ready to shift. But me... I preferred blouses and jeans until I made the change to attract Ryker.

I was wearing a pale pink sundress the day that Aidan Barrow asked me if I would meet him down at the garage where the pack vehicles are stored. It was destroyed, slashed up and covered in blood after he attacked me, and when I panicked and shifted after he tried to maneuver me into one of the open trunks, the dress was nothing but bloody tatters beneath me. I got a few swipes in with my claws and fangs before he shot me full of quicksilver—something he did repeatedly to ensure I was sedated for the whole trip to the West Coast—but that was the last time I wore one of my dresses.

While I was kept in a cage, I stayed in my fur. Only once did I shift to skin, and that's because the Wicked Wolf hit me with the full weight of his alpha stare. I couldn't refuse him, though I threatened to hurt myself if he tried to keep me from shifting back to my wolf. He had no reason to refuse. I was a pawn, a bargaining chip, a way to lure Ryker and Gem into the trap he'd set for them. I might not be able to talk while I'm a wolf, but I can hear, and I know that he only took me on the odd chance that Ryker developed some feelings for me.

After all, I spent years telling anyone who would listen that, one day, we'd be mates. I never thought it would put a target on my back, though. I just thought, if I was persistent, I could make my own happily-ever-after.

I was wrong.

I haven't thrown the sundresses away. I keep meaning to, but whenever I pull open this drawer, after my stomach tightens, my immediate reaction is to shove it closed. That's what I do now, wishing I could just remember that my blouses and t-shirts are in the next drawer down, with my jeans hanging up in my closet.

Grabbing some fresh clothes, I hurriedly get dressed. Only the promise of a breakfast I didn't have to make would get me moving this quickly, and minutes after I woke up, I'm shuffling in my bare feet toward the back door of my cabin.

I inch it open, pushing it the rest of the way when I see the covered plate sitting on my back porch. Closing my eyes, I breathe in deep. I smell bacon, yes, but that's not all.

Something musky, something woodsy, with a hint of sharp pine. Like Christmas in May, my heart skips a beat.

I know exactly who left this plate for me. And because it's from him, I can accept it without any hesitation.

So I do.

Food has a special meaning to shifters. In most packs, it's the Alpha that provides for his community.

In individual families, it's the parents' responsibility to feed their pups. That's just accepted. But when a male or a female of mating age offers food to a prospective partner, it says: I will protect you, I will feed you, and you'll want for nothing if I'm around.

Not me. I'm pretty sure I'm the only exception to that in all of Accalia.

I know the meal is from Duke. If anyone else left me a plate of—I peek under the foil—bacon and scrambled eggs, eating it is the same as signaling that I'm interested in pursuing a mating with them. It's letting another wolf take care of me. But Duke... he's been taking care of me for months now, and not because he has any kind of sexual interest in me. He treats me more like a pup that needs to be guarded and guided, and he has since the moment he found me savage and terrified in that cage in California.

Well, now I know why I woke up. It wasn't the food, was it? It was him bringing it to me. He must've just dropped it off, too, because if he'd been around longer? I never would've had the nightmare to begin with— even if it does explain why I dreamed that a massive grey wolf was rescuing me.

When Duke is near, I sleep peacefully. And when he isn't... I wish he was.

Because the big delta wolf is the only thing that keeps the bad dreams away, even if I have no idea why.

D uke Conlon.

As I dig into the still-warm breakfast, I sigh as I think of him.

Duke... that's not his real name. His real name is Jack, but last year when Gem came back to Accalia to finalize her mate bond with Ryker, she started calling him Duke for some reason. Well, no. I know why she couldn't call him Jack. That's the Wicked Wolf's first name, and I still get a shiver when I think it, too. But Duke? When I asked him after we returned home, he just shrugged and said it's what she called him and he didn't argue so it stuck.

I'm not surprised. The big delta is no match for the dominant she-wolf. It's like if Ryker told me that, instead of going by the shortened version of my name, he wanted me to only be known as Patricia. I'd be

Patricia Danvers, instead of Trish, and that would be that. So Duke's Duke now, even though I used to know him as Jack.

Well, kinda.

Unlike me, Duke isn't from Accalia. While my family being part of the Mountainside Pack goes back for generations, Duke comes from a pack of traveling wolves. Most shifter communities stay in one place, keeping their distance from humans and other supes, but there are a few packs that are nomadic. They get permission to visit other, more stable territories because they're also traders. For shifters who don't want to leave pack land, we can barter or buy from these travelers.

I never really paid attention since my parents made sure I had everything I wanted, but our old Alpha, Henry, was more than willing to up our numbers anytime he had the chance. When Duke petitioned to join the Mountainside Pack, Henry allowed it, and Duke became fast friends with Ryker and his circle.

Now he's part of the pack council, with Ryker as Alpha and Jace Burke as Beta.

He also used to be part of the foursome that serves as Gem's personal guard. After a year's absence—that still makes me feel guilty when I remember that I caused it—she returned to Accalia last summer. Right before she completed the Luna Ceremony that made her and Ryker forever mates, four wolves pledged their loyalty to her. Duke and Jace were two of them, my cousin Bobby another, and Dorian Howard was the fourth. While Ryker is responsible for the safety of the entire pack, these four wanted to make sure that his mate was protected.

Lucky Gem. An alpha female who doesn't even *need* protection, and she had four of the most strongest deltas in Accalia lining up to have her back. At the time, I was working hard to get past my jealousy. She was good enough to give permission for me to return to Accalia after Ryker banished me, and I resolved to start over. I needed to be better.

And I was... until Barrow tricked me and I ended up the political prisoner of the most feared shifter in our world.

Something happened while I was trapped in the Wolf District, though. Something changed. When Gem showed up with Jace and Duke, the big shifter voluntarily gave up his freedom so that he could be locked in the cell next to mine. I went from only knowing him as Bobby's pal, Jack, to falling asleep to his rumbled promises that he was going to make sure nothing happened to me.

He was going to keep me safe, and nothing was going to stop him from bringing me back to Accalia in one piece.

It's been seven months since he held up his end of that harshly whispered vow, and that's not all he's done, either. As if he can sense that I'm home, but I'm nowhere near whole, he's stepped back from being one of Gem's guards. Instead, he spends most of his time watching out for *me*.

I'll be the first to admit it. I'm broken. Weeks in a cage, curled up as my wolf... I didn't go completely feral, but it was close. I relied on my other half too much, and now there's this almost... disconnect between us. My wolf is there, I can sense her, but it's like I've been blocked from her. The idea of shifting has sweat forming at the base of my spine, a mournful howl building in the back of my throat. I just... I can't.

Does that mean I need a personal guard? Of course not. Trusting Barrow taught me a lesson I'll never forget, and these days I prefer to stay around my cabin. My mother makes sure my kitchen is stocked full of food so it's not like I have to leave if I don't want to. Watching me has got to be the most boring job in Accalia, but when I began to sense Duke close by my cabin more than could be explained, I finally went to the Alphas' den and met with Ryker and Gem to ask them about it.

My Alpha and his mate exchanged a look, with Gem teasing that she's grateful to have the number of her guard whittled down to three. Ryker just told me that, if I wanted him to order Duke to stay away, he would, but I didn't want that. I only wanted to understand *why* he was out there.

And, sure, I could've gone and asked him. Our time together in the cells of the Wolf District forged a bond that I don't think will ever be broken. It's not a mate bond, of course—I doubt I'll ever have one of those—but Duke kept me sane while I was on the edge of turning feral. I might be broken, but he stopped me from shattering. That's not really that surprising. Male shifters are protective of those weaker than them. He obviously thinks I need him and, well, I think I do, too.

We're friends. I guess that's what you can call us. I've never asked him why he watches me as if expecting I'll break, and we don't discuss what happened in California, but we're friends now. He brings me food when he has extra, and when he doesn't have pack duties busying him, he curls up in his wolf form outside of my cabin, keeping the nightmares at bay.

I've found him there before. I'm not sure he knows that I do—I've never mentioned it—but, sometimes when I can't sleep, I find peace watching the big grey wolf slumber on my back porch as if he doesn't have a cabin of his own. And maybe I "accidentally" left a blanket out there to make it more comfortable for him, but at least he always folds it up before he goes. The gentle giant is a man of few words, but we don't talk about his sleeping habits, either. We... we kinda don't really talk that much at all. We don't need to. It's enough just knowing he's close.

And if I wonder what it would be like to invite him to spend the night inside of my cabin with me? I quickly shove that idea out of my head. He worries for me. He feels bad that I was betrayed by my packmate, and caged by a cruel Alpha. I'm not a possible mate to him. I'm nobody.

I look down at my plate, half-empty despite my nightmare leaving me queasy.

I'm nobody—except, maybe, to Duke Conlon.

IN ACCALIA, I'M A FIXTURE. A PRETTY FIXTURE, SURE, but a fixture nonetheless.

That's... actually not new. For longer than I want to admit, that's been my life. The pretty almost-mate to Ryker, the head bitch in the group of she-wolves around my age, and one of the long-established Danvers clan. If anything, I was known for my looks and my attitude. Kind of pathetic when I look back on it now, but until the moment I was banished, I liked my life.

I had it all mapped out. I'd be the Alpha female, living in the Alpha cabin with Ryker, absolutely untouchable. Only... turns out, I became *very* touchable and for one reason only: my imagined tie to a male I never stood a chance with.

Once I was home again, I vowed that I would prove

I was more than that. That was seven months ago and I'm still trying.

It's hard. Barrow's betrayal didn't just piss off the whole pack. I fell for his lies and ended up beaten, drugged, and captured because one wolf was nice to me following my banishment. You think I would've learned my lesson after Shane Loup used me to drive a wedge between Ryker and his mate. Nope. Barrow flattered me, I believed him, and in the end I returned to Accalia with my claws and fangs blunted, my tail tucked between my legs.

My parents worry over me. I don't have any siblings, but my cousins, aunts, and uncles tried to close ranks around me before I put a stop to that. My packmates whisper. The older gammas think I had it coming, while my old friends... well, let's just say they stopped coming to see if I wanted to go for a dish and run sesh anytime soon.

Kind of hard to join a pack run when my wolf prefers to stay right where she is: far away from anyone else.

Life moves on. At least, for most of us, it does. I'm still struggling, but I'm not the only one.

And that's why, when I do want to see any of my old friends, I know there's someone in Accalia who will always welcome me.

Audrey Carter is about twelve years older than I am. Before last year we didn't really run in the same circle. She was happily mated to Grant when I was still a young pup, though her younger brother, Shane, was in the same age group as me and Ryker and a bunch of other packmates. That's how I first knew her, through Shane, and her tie to her brother is the reason why we've become so close since last summer.

In all of the pack, Audrey is the only one who understands what it's like to be an outcast. Not because of anything she did—unlike me—but because she was Shane's big sister and the only family he had when he turned on Mountainside. She blames herself for not noticing how dark he went, and when Ryker was forced to put him down, she was the only one to visibly mourn our former Beta's death.

She loved her brother, but she's as loyal to Accalia as I am. No one doubts that. Her place as one of the maternal deltas is solid. Her mate is a member of Ryker's pack circle. There's not a single shifter who blames her for what her brother did.

Except for Audrey herself, of course.

When it first came out that Shane betrayed Ryker by working with the Wicked Wolf and targeting Ryker's mate, Audrey came to visit me. Like the rest of the pack, she knew that I was helping him try to drive Gem and Ryker apart. At least, I *thought* I was helping him to keep the pack strong while also getting the male I wanted. Turns out he was manipulating me, turning me into another pawn in a convoluted plan I still don't fully understand. Either way, I was the only one who had any insight into Shane's motives.

I told her as much as I could which, admittedly, wasn't really a lot. I was too consumed with getting my own happily-ever-after to second guess why Shane thought I'd be a better mate for the Alpha than Gem to care *why* he was helping me. Looking back, I realize just how flighty and ridiculous I was. Still, making amends for my actions didn't just stop with the Alpha couple. I tried my best to support Audrey, and now she's my best friend.

She's a sweetheart. There's not an ounce of darkness in her which makes you wonder how Shane became so twisted. Just born that way, I figure. A gentle she-wolf, Audrey honestly does whatever she can to keep the morale in the pack up. Once upon a time that was going along with the pack council's plan to throw an unprepared Gem at a feral Ryker during the full moon. Nowadays, she works as the pack seamstress when she isn't doing everything she can to help out the rest of our packmates.

Including inviting me for weekly sewing lessons that couple as unofficial therapy sessions for the both of us.

I usually visit her for a lesson and lunch every Monday. Since the new year, I've learned how to darn socks, sew up any holes in a packmate's clothes that come from partial shifts, and I've even started a quilt that I'm planning on adding to my back porch. At my pace, it probably won't be done until next winter, but I think Duke would like it.

If he's still watching over me, of course.

Today's Thursday. I don't know if Audrey is busy, but after last night's bad dream, I don't want to be alone. With Duke obviously too busy to be my babysitter today, that leaves me with only a handful of choices: visiting my parents on the northern side of Accalia, visiting Bobby or Nina, my younger cousins, or seeing if Audrey is willing to keep me company until I shake off last night's shivers.

Bobby is one of Gem's trio of guards. With Jace our new Beta, and Duke... Duke, Bobby and Dorian Howard spend most of their time making sure our female Alpha doesn't do anything she isn't supposed to. Only when Ryker is with her do they back off, something I just don't understand. When I asked Bobby, he said it was a rare female alpha thing, and I decided I didn't want to know any more about it so I dropped the subject.

Ryker's not in Accalia today. Ever since rumors got out about the Luna-touched female who lives in the Fang City at the foot of our mountain, he's been spending a lot of his time going back and forth between our territory and the nearest shifter pack in River Run. Walker was killed in Muncie, and there are rumors that some of his former packmates are looking for retaliation. Add that to the group of marauding shifters who attempted to kill her, and the way she was summoned to meet with the Alpha collective— including Ryker and Gem who let Jace in charge for a couple of days—and tensions are higher than they have been lately. The vamps say they're prepared for any scuffle between supes, but the two Alphas are working to keep another Claws and Fangs war from breaking out so close to their land.

As our Alpha, the whole pack senses it when he's gone. It's easier to tolerate because Gem's still here. That's why shifter tradition has it so that a new Alpha almost always takes a mate shortly after he takes over the pack. We need balance, and an Alpha's mate provides it.

Would I have been able to? I... I thought I would. Now it doesn't matter.

On the plus side, I don't have two determined wolves dogging my every step. Just one who is conspicuously absent today.

And, no, I'm not annoyed that there's no sign of Duke at all as I get ready to leave, then take the walk over to Audrey's cabin... uh-uh. Not even a little.

Nope.

WHEN I VISIT AUDREY, WE HAVE AN UNSPOKEN agreement. I don't mention Shane anymore, and she doesn't bring up this weird... thing I have going on with Duke Conlon.

She did in the beginning. She implored me to open up to her when I felt ready to, to tell her about what happened after I went missing. Because her mate is high up in the pack's hierarchy, she knew all about how Duke is the reason I made it out of the Wolf District at all. Not as if his need to watch me is a secret. In Accalia, there aren't any, and everyone knows that I somehow triggered his protective instincts.

Too bad I didn't trigger his mating ones...

Audrey was working on hemming a dress for Flora, a newly mature she-wolf who was getting ready for her Luna Ceremony next week. Flora is a delta, and so is her intended, a shy male called Mack. To become bonded mates, they have to wait until the Luna is completely full, mate beneath her to ask for her blessing, then mark each other to prove that they choose to be bonded together forever. Unlike an Alpha's mating, there's no real ceremony. The pack congratulates every newly mated pair, but it's a private ceremony.

Still, a young female wants to look her best for her mate, and the dress Audrey is working on is perfect for the occasion.

"The soft pink will really bring out the golden notes in her eyes," I tell Audrey. "It's beautiful."

"I gave her the choice of pink or white," Audrey confides, "but after... well, most girls are going with color this season."

Right. Because Gem wore a white dress for her Luna Ceremony with Ryker, and it ended up stained in blood after the challenge from Shane that interrupted the pack-wide affair. Perfect for an alpha female, not so much for the more delicate shifters in our pack.

When I was a pup dreaming of my mating night, I imagined a mellow yellow shift dress that would complement my tanned skin, my hazel eyes, and my light brown hair. I still wear that color—most of my t-shirts and blouses are a shade of yellow—but a fancy dress... maybe not anytime soon.

Then again, it's not like I have a prospective mate, either.

I'm only twenty-seven. Shifters that grow up in the same pack as their mate usually find each other young. I didn't, which is probably another reason why I fixated on Ryker Wolfson the way I did. The whole pack knew that Ryker's mate would be from out of Accalia, just like mine would have to be. If we chose each other first, it wouldn't matter.

And then, of course, the Luna whispered that Gemma Swann was his, and I screwed up by not respecting that. Now they're mated, I'm not, and if I want to find a male to accept me, I'm going have to leave Accalia.

No, thanks.

Glancing up from her hemming, Audrey gives me a curious look. I don't know if the topic we were discussing put the idea in her head, or she just knows me pretty damn well by now, but I'm almost expecting it when she asks, "What about you, Trish? Still going lone wolf?"

I shrug. "Unless the Luna drops a male shifter in my lap who doesn't mind hooking up with Trish Danvers, it seems like that's my fate."

"That's an... interesting way of looking at it."

It's the only way I have. "It's fine. I've got time." We may not lives as long as vamps, but shifters can reach a century, easy. "If it happens, it happens. I promise I'm okay."

Audrey's a delta. An Alpha might be able to tell when their packmate is lying to them. Luckily for me, she can't.

It's my turn to change the subject now. "Now, about my quilt. I've already started attaching squares to it, but how do I finish off the ends? I was thinking—"

My words are cut short. Two familiar scents filter in through the open window of Audrey's personal den, followed by the aura belonging to a pair of delta wolves.

One is Grant Carter, Audrey's mate.

But the other...

I can't help it. Like a moth drawn to a flame, my head swivels toward the front side of her cabin.

"Aud? Audrey, honey, I stopped by to grab some lunch. Got Duke with me, too. Hope you don't mind."

I don't see Grant. Considering he mentioned lunch, he probably headed straight for the kitchen. Or maybe he's behind Duke. Luna knows even a male of Grant's build could hide easily behind Duke's bulk.

He's huge. I've never seen him naked, but I doubt there's a spare ounce of fat on him. He's got this boxer's shape and size, bulky and brawny on the top, with legs as thick as tree trunks. It's amazing how gentle and kind he can be considering he looks like he could snap even a raging, bloodthirsty vamp in half. I know first-hand that his catcher-sized mitts stroke a trembling wolf with reverence, and his eyes...

Shifters' eyes can come in all shades of browns, hazels, and golds. His are a darker hazel than mine, but there are times when the color shifts to a bright gold.

Like right now.

He's the epitome of tall, dark, and handsome. He wears his dark hair short, showing off his strong features, and I've come to realize that—now that I'm no longer obsessing over Ryker—Duke is one of the most attractive males I've ever seen before in my life.

His name is a sigh. "Hi, Duke."

"Trish? What are you..." His brow furrows. "It's not Monday."

Why am I not surprised that Duke knows that I spend my Monday afternoons at Audrey's?

Probably for the same reason that he looks confused that I'm here on a Thursday.

He's my guard. I'm the she-wolf he's been watching. Of course he knows where I am at all times.

I guess I'm predictable in that way.

Then again, I don't think he expected me to find the excuse to leave as soon as he entered the room where I was sharing a Coke and a conversation with Audrey.

"You're right. I just stopped by for a visit. I should probably be heading back to my cabin, though."

"You're leaving now?"

It seems like the best idea. It's one thing for Duke to keep an eye on me from a distance. I don't under-stand it, but I don't mind. Having him right there, fighting the pull between us that I noticed after our time in the cages? I wish I was a stronger female than I am. He's my friend, and that's all he can be.

Which I why I don't even bat an eye when he offers to walk me back to my cabin instead of joining Grant and Audrey for lunch.

I'd expect no less from such an honorable male.

"Sure. That would be nice of you."

Out of the corner of my eye, I see that Audrey is frowning. "Nice? Trish, sweetie—"

"Thanks for the drink." I stand up. "The chat, too. I'll see you on Monday."

"Um. Yeah. Okay. Take good care of her Duke."

His gaze never leaves my face as he answers in that solemn, deep voice of his, "I always will."

CHAPTER 3
SHADOW

Once we're outside of the Carters' cabin, I expect my shadow to quietly escort me back to mine.

That's what Duke is, I've long decided. My shadow. A big one, sure, since he's a giant of a male, but he doesn't often walk at my side. In fact, he usually keeps his distance, watching over me from afar.

He's done that since we returned to Accalia. As though he's expecting me to have a mental breakdown at any minute, it seems like he's always *there*. Not that it bothers me. It doesn't. My time away from the pack changed me. I'm not the she-wolf I used to be. Instead of expecting males to sniff at my tail—to which I gladly rejected them because I only wanted Ryker—I'd rather they leave me alone... except for Duke.

We don't often have conversations. It's hard to do so

when your shadow prefers to stay a good couple of feet behind, forever silent. A few stand out in my mind—nearly all of them revolving around how I'm feeling these days—but I asked him once if I should call him by his real name or his nickname. After how he took care of me, I didn't want to think of him as just another packmate. He was my friend, and I respected him.

He'd looked at me, surprise written on his ruggedly handsome face, before he rumbled out a quick, "Call me whatever ya like. What about you? Is it Patricia, or Trish?"

I'll always be Trish. But when he said *Patricia* in that bass voice of his, I couldn't help but remember the way he called my wolf the same while I was spiraling back in the cells. She had responded as if she'd been waiting for him her entire life, and though I told him, "Trish," when he asked, I admitted to myself that what he said went double. He could call me whatever he liked.

I'm the type of she-wolf who used to adore being the center of attention. Not anymore. I've had my fair share of it. In my foolish youth, I was the talk of the pack because I told anyone who would listen that I aimed to make Ryker mine, no matter what. Even after Gem left, and Ryker spent a year searching for her, I persisted even when I knew I shouldn't have. Looking back, I admit that I deserved to be banished from the pack. I got lucky to be reinstated, and luckier still that my Alpha didn't leave me to rot in California.

Rumors swirl. I know better than most that shifter packs gossip worse than little old ladies. I went from being the assumed mate for the Alpha heir to Trish Danvers, home-wrecker, in a year. Since then, I'm now damaged goods. But I'm trying to be better.

Nothing made that more clear than when Duke gave me the opportunity to call him whatever I wanted. The old Trish would've felt the need to one-up Gem, maybe give him a nickname just from me. Or I could've been contrary, referring to him as Jack since that's his name.

But I don't. I can't call him Jack—for the same reasons the Alpha female doesn't—and when it comes to Duke... it seems as if he likes the nickname; it definitely suits him. Over the last year or so, every pack-mate refers to the big male as Duke.

So I do, too.

I'm actually kind of surprised when he doesn't fall back as soon as Audrey's front door is closed. That's usually what he does, almost as if he's eager to keep some space between us, but not today. His big hand hovering an inch or so at the small of my back, he shortens his stride so that we're walking side-by-side.

He's still quiet, though, and as we start for the path that will lead us toward my cabin, I decide to break the silence for no other reason than that I like to hear his voice.

It... it does something to me. When the bad memories start to rise, or I feel the walls closing in around me like I'm still in that tiny room in California, his gentle rumble is enough to help me get past it. Not that I can admit that to him. For some reason, he already thinks he has to watch over me, even though there hasn't been any more trouble in Accalia since Walker's death. If he—or anyone—found out just how much I rely on Duke... it's not fair. It's not fair to make him responsible for a broken she-wolf he has no tie to.

If only he did...

Giving my head a small shake, I glance up at him. His expression is careful, kind of like he doesn't want to spook me.

He doesn't have to worry about that. I might have come out of my abduction a lot more aware of what dangers this world can hold, but I'll never be scared of Duke. As big as he is, as fierce as I know any wolf shifter can be, if there's one thing I'm absolutely certain of, it's that I have nothing to fear from Duke Conlon.

I give him an encouraging smile, a little surprised when his cheeks immediately go pink. "You know, you don't have to do this. I'm not too far from Audrey's."

He nods. "I know. But I'm a protector. It's my job."

Right. As one of the pack enforcers, Duke takes on

the role of protector for the rest of us. The deltas and gammas who don't want to have anything to do with pack politics or supe concerns. We live our lives in a secluded community, but we can do that because we have a powerful Alpha to lead us, and the more dominant wolves to keep us safe. Between prowling the mountain and patrolling the borders of our territory, anyone who wants to cause trouble has to go through them first.

Unless, of course, they're a pack traitor. Someone like Shane Loup or Aidan Barrow... those who smiled to your face while they were trying to figure out where the best place was to stick the silver knife in your back.

They didn't have to sneak onto the mountain. They were already here.

Another shake. Duke's brow furrows, but I change the subject quickly before he gets concerned with just how dark my thoughts are these days.

"Is that where you were last night? Pack duty?" I ask casually.

Probably a bit *too* casually.

Most decent Alphas take the safety of the pack seriously, and Ryker is no exception. There's never a moment that there aren't at least three wolves on duty, checking the border. That means overnight, too. Since Duke wasn't outside of my cabin, I just assume that he must have been on.

And doesn't that just prove that I'm still as selfish as

ever? Duke could have been anywhere. He has a small single-room cabin set on the eastern side of the mountain, and he's a high-ranking pack member. I know he's not mated, but he could still have a female he meets with in his free time.

I'm out of the loop. Before California, I never paid that much attention to any other male than the Alpha. After, whenever I thought of Duke mounting one of the unmated females in Accalia, I had a hard time controlling my claws. It got to the point that I ruined my manicure enough times when they would unsheathe without any warning that I stopped polishing my human nails.

I still have a hard time getting the image of Duke— big, brawny, handsome Duke—in bed with someone else.

Now, I've never mated myself. I had waited for Ryker to take me as his mate, and when he refused, I still held out hope he might grow desperate one full moon and settle for me anyway. The last Luna before his mating ceremony with Gem, I even followed Shane's assurance that, if I threw myself at him when the moon fever was high, he might fuck me just because I was willing.

Of course, I didn't know then that Shane was manipulating me the same way he was screwing over the pack and our Alpha. He wanted Gem for himself, and he arranged it so that I was at the Alpha cabin when she came looking for Ryker while the Luna was at her peak. But Ryker wasn't there—he was locked in the basement of his personal cabin, shifter chains restraining him from going after his mate—and that was the last chance I had before he banished me for trying to come between him and Gem.

I was only gone for a couple of weeks before I begged to be allowed back home. The next full moon, the Alphas were joined, and I was abducted a few days later. After how long I spent terrified that my first mating would be a forced one, I still haven't found a male to attempt since I've been back.

I'd never tell another soul, but last month? That was the first time I wondered if maybe... maybe Duke would be interested. He was unmated. I'm unmated. Shifters go wild when they feel the pull of the full moon, and sex is nothing if not a biological urge. Growing up, I'd heard whispers about how powerful the need could be, and I finally felt my first hint of it then.

As if I needed another reminder that I was never meant for Ryker. Pride and envy had me sure that I'd be a good match for him, and Luna knows he's a gorgeous male, but I never felt like I'd go to my hands and knees for him willingly.

But when I look at Duke—

Whoa. I'm looking at him now.

More importantly, he's looking at *me.*

"Yeah, actually. I wasn't supposed to do the overnight, but Benjy's pup had her first shift. He was celebrating with his mate, so I took over for him." He pauses, his forehead furrowed. "Why did you ask?"

"Uh." Crap. How am I supposed to answer?

"Are you... did you need me?"

Double crap. I don't want Duke to think that he *has* to take care of me. That's something I'd only ever expect from a mate, and I've given up hope that there's some male in Accalia who wants to put up with what it means to choose Trish Danvers as his.

So I shrug. "Sometimes you're there. Sometimes you're not. I just noticed you weren't, that's all."

It's not all. See? This is why I go along with his choosing to stay quiet. I open my mouth, I say something that would have been better left unsaid.

"Oh, Trish... you had another nightmare, didn't you?"

And I just did it again.

Good thing that being a she-wolf means that I'm quick on my feet. When Duke's soft murmur reaches me, I stumble over my feet, but I regain my balance before I land on my butt.

Duke's quick, too. Though I sense his hand moving to steady me, he pulls back before his skin makes contact with mine. That's a surefire way to insult a supe, and unless I give him permission to touch me, I could lash out at him if he catches me off guard.

Would I? I... I don't know. Not on purpose. Not to Duke.

But I might. Especially now that he's mentioned my nightmare.

How does he know? We can pretend that he doesn't spend most nights sleeping outside on my porch and that I have no clue he's out there. His lingering scent and the blanket I leave for him make it obvious that's bullshit. I feel safer having him close, and he's right. He's a protector to his core.

I never told him about my nightmares, though. So how does he know?

"Duke—"

"It's okay. It won't happen again. I'll ask Ryker to keep me off of the overnights."

"What? No. I don't... you don't have to do that."

"And like I told you before, I know. But unless you ask me not to, I'm going to do it anyway." He waits a beat, before rumbling, "So? Are you going to ask me?"

I'm not, and we both know it. If I wanted him to leave me alone, I would've marked my immediate territory last September, made it clear that he wasn't welcome so close. No male shifter could sleep on a she-wolf's porch without her permission, express or otherwise. I want him there. I just wish he had a different reason to stay with me than the one he has.

Pity.

As if I could pretend otherwise. Nope, especially

when he clears his throat and says, "Have you shifted recently? Let your wolf out for a run?"

When my gaze drops to the dirt, he makes a sympathetic sound in the back of his throat. "It'll do you good, Trish. If you get in touch with your wolf, it might stop the nightmares."

Right. The nightmares where I'm trapped in my fur again, with the Wicked Wolf chasing me.

"I never said I had any nightmares," I tell him. "Besides, I'm fine. I'm home. I'm safe."

And Walker's dead. He can never hurt me again.

"You are," he says, a finality to the two words that chases the dread settling in my gut away... for the moment, at least. "But... I've been thinking. Maybe you should visit Dahlia. She might be able to help you more than I can."

I dare a glance up at him. Instead of the pity I expect, his expression has turned earnest.

That's the only reason that I decide to be honest and admit, "I have. And you're right. She helps a lot, but I'm not the only shifter in Accalia. I can't monopolize all of her time."

Dahlia is our Omega. Her rank of wolf is the glue that holds a pack together. Like a therapist in the human world, just talking to the spiky-haired, blonde wolf leaves you feeling a bit more at peace than you did before. She's also a schoolteacher for the young pups, so there are a lot of calls on her time. She's kind enough to see me when she can—and, I admit, it's probably more due to her good-hearted, omega nature than because any of my packmates think Trish Danvers is worthy of their sympathy—and, like Duke, Dahlia helps keep the nightmares away for a while.

When Gem first came to join our pack, everyone believed she was another omega. She'd been pretending to be one her entire life, and because her dominance was so different than any other rank-and-file she-wolf, it made sense she was an omega. The only other female alpha in shifter tradition was our revered goddess, the Luna herself. No one ever guessed she could be the second—but Shane knew. He knew, and he told me, and I used Gem's hidden secret to blackmail Ryker into rejecting her.

I can't change what I've done. I can only admit that I was wrong, and try to be better in the future. Dahlia is our only Omega. With Gem, we thought we'd have a second, but we don't. I'm not the only one who needs Dahlia's wolf to deal with my own demons.

That's why, when Duke says, "You need her. It's not monopolizing anything if you need her more," I shake my head.

"Why not?"

My knee-jerk reaction is to tell the truth. "Because I'm not important enough."

"Of course you are."

"That's sweet, Duke, but I know what I am. Who I am."

"So do I."

That has my head finally looking up again. As we continued to walk, I'd avoided meeting his eyes as we drew up to my cabin, but when Duke's voice goes impossibly deep, I have to see if I imagined what I heard.

I... I don't think I did.

His eyes have melted to a soft golden shade. His jaw is chiseled, his features hard, but there's a sudden gentleness to them as he tucks his chin into his chest, making it easier for him to stare directly into my face.

He lifts his hand. I can feel the heat pouring off of his fingers as he ghosts his thumb over my cheek. He never makes contact, but he doesn't have to. I shiver anyway.

"What?" I ask.

It's a squeak. The word slips out, but I couldn't keep it back. It was impossible. There's promise written in every line of his face, a promise that reminds me of the fierce Duke who reached past the silver bars, burning his human arm raw just to stroke my fur, reminding me that he was there—and that he would do anything to bring me home again.

My cabin is behind me. Somehow, Duke is closer than we've been in months. My heart is racing, my wolf up and keening as she recognizes something in his golden gaze that my human half just can't understand.

And then he murmurs, "You're important to me."

I blink. My lips part, but I don't have any idea what to say to that.

Later on, I still won't be sure if the emotions of the moment made me read more into his intentions than were truly there. His eyes drop from mine down to my lips, his chin jerking forward. I get the sudden feeling that he's about to kiss me, and I freeze like a deer in front of a predatory shifter.

Maybe he was. Then again, maybe he finally noticed how close we were all of a sudden and he was about to back away. I'll never know because, like that very same deer confronted with a hungry wolf, I choose to flee.

Duke doesn't chase. When I take a few hurried steps back, then bolt for my door, he stays exactly where I left him.

About ten feet separate us. As I try to slow my racing heart, I lift up a hand. "Good night."

He does the same. "Sweet dreams."

Right now, I'd rather not have any at all.

With a quick wave, I let myself into my cabin. And though I can still sense his bold, comforting aura just outside of my territory, I turn the lock on the door and let out the breath I hadn't even realized I was holding.

CHAPTER 4
LOCKS

The locks should've been my first clue that I'm not okay.

We don't lock our cabins in Accalia. There's no reason to. You should be able to trust your packmates or the whole idea of living in a shifter community, sharing goods and wealth, providing for the next generation of pups... it's bullshit. Shifters are hard-wired to live together and support each other. Those that aren't either choose to be a lone wolf or go feral.

And then there are the bad seeds like Shane Loup. A beta who wanted nothing more than to be an alpha, he acted the role of the perfect packmate all while working behind our backs. Worse, I *helped* him.

I want to think I'm not like him. Hurting my pack was never part of my plan. I honestly believed that, as

Ryker's mate, I'd make it better. We didn't need an outsider she-wolf coming in to join with him, especially when I believed she was an omega. Having a rare female alpha take the top spot would be a coup for any shifter pack, but she came with baggage. The Wicked Wolf wanted her, and so did Shane. If I got Ryker out of the deal, I didn't care—so long as Mountainside was safe.

But it wasn't. At least, not for me. Because of everything I've done, I put a target on my back. It might be gone now, but the illusion of safety that hung over my cabin, the trees, and the mountains I've lived on my whole life... it's gone, and I don't know if I'll ever get it back.

Logically, I know that the locks won't do shit. A shifter's brute strength would snap the doorknob right off if they really wanted to get to me. Still, for the same reason I keep my windows closed, I lock the doors behind me anytime I return to my cabin. It's something small that makes me feel better, and anyone with good intentions would respect my need for security these days.

I just wish I could go back to the way I used to be. Carefree and flippant, a quick tongue and a satisfied smile... that's the old Trish. The new Trish takes a deep breath before checking the door one final time, then retreating to the kitchen for a small snack to settle her nervous stomach.

Maybe Duke's right. In the first few weeks after I returned from California, I saw Dahlia every couple of days. Both my Alpha and my parents insisted on it, and I was so screwed up that I snarled at them to leave me alone. I was like a wounded animal backed into a corner, even in my skin, and I almost attempted to challenge the three shifters who had any authority over me and my wolf.

Luckily, they didn't take me up on it. My parents never would, no matter how much I snapped my fangs at them, and Ryker... he's a good male, and a better Alpha. He arrived in the Wolf District shortly before the whole Western Pack imploded, so he was there to see what the quicksilver sedative and the silver cell did to me. Duke, too. I'll never forget how he actually stood between me and Ryker, daring to meet our Alpha's eyes, warning him that he wouldn't be ordered to stand down until *I* gave the command for him to.

That's how I ended up riding in the backseat of the rented car with Duke while Gem drove and Ryker sat shotgun. Halfway home, I finally felt secure enough to shift back. Forever the gentleman, Duke immediately closed his eyes. Gem barked at Ryker to do the same, which I get. Nudity isn't a big deal in a pack, but I had made a move on her male before. I couldn't expect her to forget that. As for Duke... he's just a good guy. Of course he wouldn't peek, even if it didn't mean anything to him.

He did, however, offer me a shift dress he grabbed with him before we left the Wolf District. Simpler than the sundresses I used to wear, it covered me up until we made our way back home.

I thought that would be the last time he took care of me. Nope. Seven months later, he still is. I don't know how to tell him that, while Dahlia's wolf has soothed some of the jagged edges inside of me, it's a delta who's done the most work putting me back together.

So maybe I should visit her again. It's been a couple of weeks since I have, but when Duke's wolf does even more to stop the nightmares and the bad memories and the countless what-ifs from racing through my mind... I'd rather rely on him.

It isn't fair. I know that. I'm putting too much pressure on a male who I'd talked to maybe twice before he saved me from the lowest point in my life. The way I see it, though, he doesn't have to. He says it's his job. He's a protector for the Mountainside Pack.

And, well, I'm a packmate, aren't I?

It's a flimsy justification at best. I don't care. For as long as he wants to be my shadow, I'll let him. It's the closest I've ever had to anyone being mine.

If only he was for real.

WHEN I FINALLY FALL ASLEEP MUCH LATER THAT NIGHT, I expect the nightmares to follow me. Most days I can shove my past behind me. It's something I've always been good at. I used to be able to shake off the day, no matter what, and still have a pleasant night's sleep.

Not anymore.

It's probably not the healthiest coping mechanism, but I still try. If I don't think about what happened after Barrow first turned on me, or when Walker's dark, menacing aura would visit me in the cells, threatening me more effectively than the words the cruel Alpha tossed my way, then I can pretend I'm the old Trish again. It never lasts for long, but it's worse when I fall back into the spiral of reliving those awful moments.

Barrow was a kid, barely twenty, and he sliced me to ribbons before injecting me with enough quicksilver that my hold on my wolf has never been the same. Walker told me that I'd be another one of his personal bitches, a willing pussy whenever he wanted it, because my Alpha all but threw me away. If Ryker didn't come, I'd be passed along to any male who wanted me, and maybe then I could see how long I'd stay so pretty...

Even dead, his threats still haunt me the same way his golden wolf chases me into my dreams. I can never escape him—except for when I sense the comforting energy of a protective wolf who will never, ever harm me.

I sleep dreamlessly for a few hours before I wake up suddenly. It's pitch dark in my cabin, and I reach out instinctively. It's such a subconscious act, one I do without even really meaning to, and when my wolf follows an invisible thread and finds Duke's waiting at the end of it, I sit up.

I don't know why I'm so surprised that he's out there. Sure, I left him standing off the edge of my porch after that strangely charged moment between us, but he's the one who mentioned my nightmares. If he somehow figured out that I suffer from them when he's out patrolling Accalia at night, if he wasn't on duty now, of course he'd stick around.

That's what a decent protector like Duke Conlon does.

I don't know why I start to climb out of bed. Or maybe I do, but I want to blame my sleepy state for what happens next. It doesn't matter either way. My wolf whines, imploring me to go to his, and after I snag my blanket off of my rumpled sheets and shrug on a nightgown, that's exactly what I do.

Tip-toeing on my bare feet, I know instinctively that he's still out back. I push open the door and immediately find him.

In his human form, Duke stands above a crowd. He's no different when he's shifted to his fur. Dark grey and massive, he sprawls out over nearly the entire length of the blanket I leave outside for nights like these. He's on his side, legs stretched out in front of him, belly falling and rising in time to his chuffing breaths.

He's dead asleep. Knocked out to the world. I have no doubt in my mind that, if a threat approached, he'd flip like a switch, waking up to confront it with barely a missed step. But since it's just me and him and the trees that surround the back of my cabin, he sleeps on while I look my fill.

I should go back inside. He's here, and that means that the nightmares won't find me tonight. But then I remember the look in his eyes I swore I saw before I bolted. His gentle rumble, the way he told me I was important to him... and I close the door behind me before stepping lightly over to him.

Duke snuffles, but his wolf doesn't stir. Not even when I drop to my knees, then cozy up against him. I prop my back up against his bulk, turning my face into his sleek fur. This close, the pine scent is stronger than ever. I breathe in deep, letting it settle over me.

In the Wolf District, we had bars between us. Walker's people allowed Duke to stay with me, just not in my personal cell. That didn't stop him from trying any way to make some physical contact between us, even if the silver burned him over and over again. He wanted me to know I wasn't alone.

As I drift off to sleep, soothed by the sounds of his wolf deep in slumber, I do the same for the big delta.

No matter what happens, at least one good thing came out of my captivity.

We have each other.

I'M UP BEFORE DUKE. GOOD THING, TOO, BECAUSE I'M bare-assed naked.

It's the whisper of the breeze against my over-heated skin that tickles me awake. I stretch, and it takes me a second to realize that his fur is cradling my bare back, and my nightgown is gone.

Not only that, but my muscles don't feel tight anymore. The slight headache—a rarity for a supe—I'd been battling for days has disappeared. In fact, I feel better than I have in a while.

And that's because I... I shifted.

It's obvious. When a shifter goes too long between changing forms, we pay for it. In a world full of humans who have no idea that supes exist, it's a given that we spend more time in our skin. Throw in the fact that we communicate better with words than howls, and shifters don't fuck in the fur, and our two-legged shape is the default.

But we're shifters. We need to shift. If our wolf doesn't get their fair share of being in control, we get antsy. Our skin itches, then our muscles clench. We get stomachaches. Headaches. Fatigue. All signs that our body needs to change shapes, but ones I purposely ignored for way too long.

A laugh bubbles up inside of me, one that I swallow as I scoot to my knees, looking at the disturbed grass beneath my legs. The grass is torn up, my feet muddy. I must've shifted, then dug in the dirt with my paws before circling around and falling back asleep with Duke. At some point, I shifted back to human—obviously—but that doesn't change the fact that I did it. I shifted.

Now that I've gone wolf again, I can admit my deepest, darkest shame: I was afraid that I'd never be able to let her out again with struggling.

It's the quicksilver that fucked me up. I don't know if my reaction is usual. Though Audrey's not proud of what she did, she only served a couple of drops to Gem in a doctored glass of Coke. Enough to sedate the powerful alpha female, but there was no harm done. Within a couple of hours it wore off, and that gave the pack council time to escort her to Ryker's cabin.

They didn't shoot her up with it like Barrow did me. She got a couple of drops. I got two or three doses a day during travel so that I was a groggy, frightened mess when I woke up in the Wolf District, completely naked and cut off from my wolf.

Walker's people gave me a shift dress when they brought me to the cell that would be my home for the next few weeks, but the second I could finally tap into my other half again, I shredded that thing before shifting to my fur.

I refused to shift back. Let them think I was an animal. During my stay, I *was*—

—until Duke found me. Until a piece of home chose to sit at my side, soothing me with his bass voice, promising me everything and nothing if I could maintain my tenuous grip on my sanity. I did. Barely, but I did.

The quicksilver has been out of my system for a long, long time. I sense my wolf in every breath, every sigh, every beat of my Luna-damned heart. Still, she didn't want to come out. It wasn't just me. It was both of us. She needed the time to heal, to lick her wounds, and I needed to prove that I was me again. Trish.

Now, though? With the proof of my latest shift around me—literally, as my nightgown is scattered pieces of fabric dusted over our blankets—I finally feel whole.

And I have Duke to thank for that.

I doubt he'd see it that way. All he did was play the role of my guard, sleeping on my back porch so that my wolf sensed his and knew she was safe. I might have taken advantage of his kindness to curl up next to him, but I was in my skin when I did that. I haven't sleep-shifted in years, but wrapped up in Duke's aura, I did.

I'm still broken... just not beyond repair. I can shift again.

I'm whole.

Another laugh escapes me. For the first time in forever, I feel light. Free. It's like a weight I hadn't even realized I'd been carrying was lifted from my shoulder. I want to bounce. I want to run. I want to drop to all fours, give control over to my other side, throw back my head, and howl in shuddering relief.

I don't, though, if only because Duke is still slumbering where I left him. I can care less if I wake up all of Accalia... just not him. He sleeps like a hibernating bear, rumbling and snorting, but I know it's because he spends more hours a day protecting our pack—protecting *me*—than he can even make up in a couple of short naps. If he's resting, sleeping through me joining him outside *and* sleep-shifting... well, I'm not going to disturb him.

But I will do something.

I wait until I've put enough distance between us by crawling to hop to my feet and hurry for my porch. So giddy, I don't even stop to lock the door. I just race for my room, grabbing the first change of clothing that I find, all while my brain is whirling.

He does so much for me. I don't care if it's because of his role as protector. So many of my packmates gave up on me after the trouble I caused. I don't blame them, but the truth is what it is. Duke could've abandoned me, too. He didn't, though, and it's about time I show him how much I appreciate it—and how much I've grown to care about him.

I'm a shifter. There's only one way I can do that and make sure he gets my meaning.

With food.

CHAPTER 5
CUPCAKES

y mother is giddy when I ask her to get me all of the ingredients I need to make cupcakes.

I'll be the first to admit I was a late bloomer. It's part of the reason why I didn't even think about who I would take as a mate until I was twenty. I was too distracted when I was young, no one really caught my attention as a "practice" mate, and I had a hobby that I preferred when I wasn't hanging around with the other she-wolves.

As a pup, I spent a lot of time in the kitchen because my beloved grandmother used to bake breads and pastries for the pack. For a while, I entertained the idea of taking over for her when she retired. It wasn't long before I realized I couldn't bake bread for shit, and I didn't have the patience for fiddly pastries like choux and puff.

But, Luna, could I make a mean cupcake.

When you're a pup, you can feed anyone and there is no hidden meaning to it. As I got older, I couldn't just bake cupcakes for fun, only if I was serving them to family and my girlfriends; no innuendo there. Males would think differently unless I was the pack baker.

However, before I could decide if that's what I wanted to do, I fell for Ryker. Hard. I should've known then that, if my cupcakes couldn't sway him, *I* never could, but from twenty on, I only baked for him. When he refused to take them, I stopped baking at all.

Mom tried to see if I wanted to start up again after my banishment was lifted. Same story when I came back from the Wolf District. She remembered how happy I was when I was creating recipes for the tiny cakes and decorating them with frosting and fondant designs. In her kind way, she thought she could bring the old Trish—the good Trish—back with some flour, sugar, and butter.

It didn't work. I can't tell you the last time I pulled my mixer out of storage. It wasn't something that interested me—until I have the impulse to bake a dozen for Duke Conlon.

I don't tell her who I'm making them for, of course. Knowing my parents as I do, they'll get it in their heads that, this time, Duke might be the one for me. They've

58

been pushing me to search out a chosen mate these last couple of years, and I'm sure they'd be ecstatic if it was a respected council member strong enough to protect their only pup.

Or, Luna help me, they might get the idea in their skulls that Duke might even be the *one*. My fated mate.

Yeah, right.

He can't be. I would know. Even if I'm too screwed up to recognize my forever standing there in front of me, he'd have some kind of clue. It's instinct.

Not that it matters. Even if we're not fated, we could be mates, and I don't want to give my poor parents the impression when that's not how Duke sees me at all. Because, while an alpha wolf is usually blessed with the identity of his mate, regular deltas aren't. We either luck out on finding our fated mate or we don't. But since we're also not solitary creatures, we make the best of it and choose a mate instead.

He could have anyone.

Though, as I start setting the ingredients out, muscle memory taking over as the familiar scents of vanilla and sugar, baking powder and butter fill my cozy kitchen... I have to ask myself: why not me?

Now, he's not my fated mate. I'm fairly sure of that. I've known of him for years, and have gotten closer and closer in the last seven months. If he was, there should've been some sign that we were meant for each other. Some kind of bond building between us.

Sorry, I don't count the trauma bond, or his need to protect me even now that we're home. So, no. He's not my fated mate.

Duke's never made any move like I could be his, either. I'm probably being ridiculous, mistaking my gratitude and affection for something else... but all the way up until I'm standing outside of Duke's cabin, a dozen cupcakes in my trembling grasp, I can't help but wonder: what if?

I know he's home. I can sense his comforting aura like a warm blanket on a chilly mountain night even from twenty yards away. I'd taken a chance, hoping he'd be at his cabin instead of on patrol—and that he'd be alone—but I've always been impulsive.

It took everything I had to wait until the cupcakes were cool enough to decorate them, and even longer for the frosting to set before I could transport them through the woods. By the time Duke opens the door, my wolf is almost whining, looking for some sign that he is pleased by my token.

One thing for sure, the puzzled look on Duke's face when he sees me standing there definitely isn't one.

"Trish? What are you doing here?"

He sounds guarded. Wary. Makes sense. He must've figured out that I'd snuck out to sleep by his wolf last night, but it was equally obvious that I left him before he woke up. So focused on planning what kind of cupcakes I was going to make, I didn't even think to offer him some breakfast. As if nothing was different, I walked away, and he did the same when he got up.

But something *was* different. I felt it when my wolf shifted for the first time in ages, and it only became undeniable as I was baking. Whatever relationship we have, I don't want Duke to go back to being the silent shadow in the distance. For good or for bad, we have a tie forged in silver, and I need to respect that.

Starting with making him an offering of his own.

"I made you something." Holding the cupcake platter out to Duke, I say, "Here. These are for you."

At first, he doesn't take it. My heart sinks all the way down to my feet when all Duke does is stare at the twelve frosted cupcakes as if he can't believe what he's seeing.

"What's this?"

"You're always bringing me food. I thought it was about time I did the same."

Everyone knows what it means when a shifter provides food for another. For so long, I've accepted that I was the only exception... but I don't want Duke to be. I want him to take these cupcakes from me and know that I'm saying: I will feed you, I will love you, and you'll want for nothing while I'm around.

I wait on a bated breath to see if he will, swallowing the sound of relief when he does with a solemn, "That was nice of you."

Screw nice. "If you say so."

Him accepting them isn't enough. For my wolf to be satisfied, he has to actually take a bite.

"Go on." I use my chin to gesture at the tray. "Aren't you going to eat them? Have a bite?"

"I will. Later. Thank you. I... thanks."

Standing there, Duke awkwardly holding onto the platter, I realize that there was nothing else to do. Unless I decide to climb him like a tree and shove one of my cupcakes into his mouth, I can't force him to eat them if he doesn't want to. I just have to hope he does.

I smile, though my heart's not quite in it. For a female who spent years being endlessly rejected by the male she chased, you'd think I'd be used to it. I'm not. And, Luna, it's especially worse when I thought I might... I might have found someone else who would accept me for me.

I guess I was the one reading way too much into it.

I SHOULDN'T BE DISAPPOINTED. TELL THAT TO MY WOLF.

The whole way back to my cabin she was laying flat on her belly, paws forward, muzzle resting on her legs. I almost want to mimic her pose. The high from shifting last night has come crashing down on me, all because I saw something that wasn't there and made a foolish, rash decision to act on it.

Like I said. I should've known better.

After I enter my cabin, locking the door behind me like usual, I do the routine check to make sure no one came inside while I was gone; without a key, I can't lock up when I go, though even pouting, my wolf is strong enough to sense any intruder upon my return. I frown when I see the mess I left behind in the kitchen. So excited to bring my cupcakes to Duke, I left the bowls and dishes and half-filled piping bag where they were.

I don't have the energy to clean up yet. Like my wolf, I'd rather throw myself a pity party I don't deserve. So, retreating to my bedroom, I do exactly that. Kicking off my shoes, I plop down on my bed and rest my eyes.

Claws crossed that I don't fall asleep. Mood I'm in following Duke's rejection, I wouldn't be surprised if I have a doozy of a nightmare.

Luckily, I don't, even if I do knock out. I nap for the next few hours, finding solace in my loneliness and dreamless sleep. I might even have gone without dinner and slept right through the night if it wasn't for the fact that, shortly before dark, there comes a banging at my front door.

I hear it first, heart leaping into my throat as my eyes spring wide open. The rest of my senses come online seconds later. Once I catch the scent of the delta male outside, I understand why my wolf didn't warn me of his approach. That's family out there, and no matter how messed up I am, I'm not afraid of family.

Bang.

Bang.

"Trish? I know you're in there!"

Bang.

Rolling my eyes, I glance down to make sure that I didn't sleep-shift again. Nope. I'm still wearing the same blouse and jeans from earlier today so I don't have to worry about hearing Bobby complain that I've scarred him for life by prancing around naked in front of my cousin.

"Trish!"

"Hold on," I holler back. "I'm coming!"

To my reply, the idiot bangs on my door again.

I swear, there better be an emergency in Accalia for all the racket he's making. Like, honestly, I need him to warn me that we're under attack, or one of Walker's not-dead Betas found us, or Aleksander Filan decided to wage war on the Mountainside Pack. Something like that.

I definitely don't expect him to march into my cabin once I unlock the door and wave an empty cupcake wrapper in front of my face.

"I can't believe you did this to me! I stood up for you. When Walker had Barrows grab you, I pleaded with the Alpha to find some way to bring you home safe. And how do you repay me? With betrayal!"

You know, everyone else in Accalia handles me with kid gloves. My parents. Duke. Even Audrey.

Not Bobby Danvers.

I roll my eyes. "What are you talking about?"

"Duke's my pal. You're family. I didn't get involved because you two have got to work this out yourself, but that's before you brought cupcakes into it."

"Again, I ask: what are you talking about?"

This time, I'm referring to the first part of what he said—you two have got to work this out yourselves—but Bobby is still only irrationally focused on the last bit.

"Cupcakes!" The youngest Danvers of this generation, he's always been the one closest to his wolf. As he snaps out the word, I see his canine teeth have become fangs. "I stopped by Duke's and smelled the buttercream. And do you know what I found?"

I'm pretty sure he's going to tell me.

He waves the wrapper again. "This! This was all that was left!"

What?

"One wrapper? But I made him a whole dozen."

"Yeah. I *know*. I saw all of the wrappers, but this is the only one I got before he ran me out of his cabin. He ate them all and got snappish when I asked for a wrapper to lick the icing. Can you believe it?"

Um. No, actually. I can't.

I go warm. My whole body... it heats up with pleasure.

Because Duke? He ate the cupcakes. He ate all twelve.

He ate my food.

I don't care what the big delta thinks it means. To me, it means something particular.

It means... it means I might have a chance. A small one, sure, but a chance is a chance—and I've done way more with less.

Bobby is still ranting and raving. My toes are just about curling against the wooden floor of my cabin, and he's still complaining about selfish enforcers and betraying relatives.

"If you're baking again, you can make me some, too," he says. "I'm your cousin. Family. Until the two of you get your act together, I should come first."

Maybe. Maybe he's right. Maybe Duke and I do need to get our act together.

And maybe I should thank Bobby for coming here to tell me because, Luna knows, I'm not so sure Duke ever would... well, not yet, at least.

I hold up my hand.

Pack council or not. Protector of the alpha female or not. Dominant shifter or not... Bobby is my younger cousin. I have some sway. He clicks his fangs together, waiting for me to say something.

That's why, feeling generous, I wave toward my

kitchen. "If you stop talking right now, you can lick the beaters. There's still some batter in the bowl from this morning, and the piping bag of buttercream should still be fresh. Knock yourself out."

Bobby yips, then lunges for me, smacking a kiss on my cheek. "Thanks, Trish. You're the best!"

I'm not. But I'm trying my hardest to be.

IF MY WAY TO EVEN OUT SOME OF THE POWER IMBALANCE between us is by baking Duke a dozen cupcakes every day, then that's what I'm going to do. It might not be much—especially since he continues to sleep outside of my cabin, with or without me—but it feels like something to me.

We do this for about three days before he finally eats one in my company. I don't leave until he tells me what he thinks about them, and after he says it was the best cupcake he's ever had, I can't help myself. I throw my arms around his side and squeeze as much of him as I can.

Hugging Duke Conlon is like hugging a tree, only softer and infinitely hotter.

Speaking of heat...

This afternoon, I used my baking session as a way to distract myself more than anything. The warmth I felt a couple of days ago hasn't faded yet. In fact, it's only grown stronger. Heat pouring off of the oven has me exchanging my normal clothes for a simple shift dress. Nothing as extravagant as my old collection of sundresses, the shift dress is more like a slip than anything else. No underwear, either, since it's chafing my skin.

I'm not just overheated. I'm overstimulated.

While the cupcakes are baking, I take a cold shower and bring myself to come twice before the timer goes off. It doesn't help. In fact, it just makes me realize how... how *empty* I feel.

Like everything would be okay if I found something hard and thick and sturdy to shove up inside of my aching pussy.

My freshly washed hands are shaking as I'm icing the cupcakes. Sweat builds at the base of my neck. I scoop my shower-damp hair over my shoulder, wiping it away with my wrist. It doesn't help, though the contact makes me realize that I don't just feel hot on the inside.

I'm really burning up.

Talk about denial. It isn't until I step out onto my porch, clutching my platter of cupcakes like a lifeline as I notice that tonight is the night of the Luna, that I realize what's wrong with me.

This is moon fever, and I'm already lost to it.

I guess it makes sense. Mature shifters feel the need to mate—and Luna knows I have—but they can... handle it on their own if there's no partner for them to choose. If there is, if there's someone our wolf will accept, the Luna's pull makes it so that it's harder to refuse.

And when you go against the Luna's wishes... she makes you pay with the fever.

There's only one way I can treat it. Find the male my wolf would welcome and entice him to mate.

Too bad I don't have any idea how to do that.

It's supposed to be instinct. Like so much of being a shifter, we do what we feel is right—but that got me in trouble before. Relying on my own wants and desires ruined my life. I'm not about to ruin an innocent male's, too.

Of course, if I bring these cupcakes to Duke's on the night of the full moon and one thing leads to another... well, you can't blame a she-wolf for that, can you?

Apparently, I discover, you can. At least, your cousin can.

I don't know if he guessed I would make a move on his friend or not, but Bobby waylays me just outside of Duke's cabin. For a moment, I think about accusing him of cock-blocking me—or maybe bribing him with Duke's cupcakes—and that's when I notice the grim expression on his usually easygoing face.

"Let me stop you right here, Trish. Go home. Wait

out the full moon where it's safe. And, Luna help me, keep your doors locked."

Right. Because with my newly developed para-noias, the last thing I need is for my protector cousin to tell me it's a good idea to lock my doors.

"Okay. I will," I tell him, if only because he looks like he won't take no for an answer, "but I just want to drop these cupcakes off to Duke first."

"You can't."

"Bobby—"

"You don't want to see him. Not tonight. Trust me."

He's a Danvers. Of course I do.

That doesn't stop me. "I'll leave them on his porch. I won't even see him."

But if Duke sees me...

Bobby shakes his head. "You'd be wasting your time. He's not even there."

"How do you know that?"

Bobby runs his fingers through his hair, claws leaving track marks in their wake. I can tell he doesn't want to answer me—but after a few moments, he does.

Probably because I threatened to never make him another cupcake again as long as he lived. Oh, well. It does the job.

"Ah, Luna, Trish. It's 'cause he went off to borrow the Alpha's chains."

C hains.

Every pack has a pair. Forged from silver, they're absolutely unbreakable. All supes react to silver, and shifters are no exception. It weakens us—a fact I know all too well after my time in a cage lined with silver bars—and it burns our skin raw if we touch it.

No shifter will choose to put on a pair of chains unless there is no other option. They're for ferals, mainly, or those who aren't too sure of their control.

Everyone in Accalia knows the rumors about Ryker and the chains. I hate to admit that I know for sure that they're not rumors, and our Alpha spent every night of the full moon chained in his cabin's basement because he was a danger to the rest of us.

He was a shifter without his true mate, and for a

whole year, he didn't know where Gem was hiding out. Their bond was strained, magic covering up her scent, and he had no way to track her since it seemed as if she'd just disappeared. No one knew she was insane enough to risk death by fang in Muncie—or that she survived, the only shifter living in the Fang City. Ryker's wolf still wanted his mate, though, and he would've burned the whole world down to get to her if he could.

The chains were essential. When the moon fever hit him, not even an alpha wolf could break through the mystically forged silver chains. His pack council set him free the next morning, and we all agreed to pretend that it wasn't happening. Alphas need complete faith and loyalty to lead their pack, and none of Mountainside wanted their pity for Ryker's unfortunate situation to get in the way of that.

If he felt anything like I have tonight, I put him through torture. Tomorrow, when the fever breaks, I'll experience guilt for my actions all over again. But tonight? All I can think about is how my wolf picked one male for me to entice—and he needs the Alpha's chains.

There's only one reason why he would: Duke is a shifter without his mate.

I've known him for seven months. More, really, but our friendship only began those awful days in California. He's never once mentioned that he has a mate. No one in Accalia has. As far as I know, he's unmated, just like me. No female would stand by and allow their mate to protect another she-wolf, no matter what his position in the pack is.

So maybe he doesn't have a mate—but he has an intended. A female his body and wolf believe is his, and who he'd be with if he could. Since he can't, he's choosing chains and a night of agony in Ryker's old basement.

Makes sense. Only a handful of cabins have the underground rooms to begin with. From the rumors that have whispered through the pack's gossip mill, Ryker's chains were big and heavy, but also screwed into the cinder block wall in his basement. They're not something that Duke could bring to his single-room cabin. He has to be there.

When I walk away from my cousin, my thoughts spinning like a top, I'm sure he expects me to return to my cabin. I make sure to head in that direction until I'm out of sight, then quickly start sprinting through the trees. Good thing I left the cupcakes with Bobby so that my arms are free to pump as I run.

Before he was the Alpha, Ryker was the Alpha heir. He was still high up in the pack that the cabin he took after he became a mature male was on the outskirts of Accalia, on the opposite side of where his parents' cabin stood. If I take the right path, I can make it there without any of my packmates figuring out where I've gone.

Only Bobby knows that I was looking for Duke tonight. So many other of my fellow shifters will be with their own mates. What do they care if I follow through with my plan to see if he'd be interested in having sex with me?

I'm sure his intended mate would care. But, see, that just proves that old, selfish Trish will never be gone and buried, no matter how hard I try. I want Duke. Forever would be nice, but I'll take just tonight if I can. He doesn't have to agree. He can stay true to his intended if he wants, but I wouldn't be Trish Danvers if I didn't at least give him the option to choose me.

No one in Accalia locks the doors, except for me. Even on the night of the full moon, with the Luna running him ragged and leading him to reach for Ryker's chains, Duke leaves the front door unlocked.

The basement door, too.

I let myself in quickly. Because I'm me, I do lock the door, and because I don't want anyone distracting us, I drag a chair in front of it, too. A determined shifter could still get inside, but at least I made it a little harder for them.

A howl erupts from below my feet. I can't tell if

Duke knows I'm the one moving back and forth over his head or not, but the pain in the howl is enough for me to give up on barricading the door further. That's the keening cry of a wolf in need, and mine is here to answer the call.

Hurrying for the basement door, I take a deep breath on the first stair, then step lightly down the entire flight.

"Oh, Duke..."

If I had any reservations about my selfish plan, they're shot to hell when I see big, strong Duke Conlon crumpled on the floor.

No shirt. No shoes. His jeans are torn in a couple of places from where his body started a partial shift before the silver in the chains affected him, and his head is hanging on his neck. He's breathing hard, and when his head jerks up, as though he's just caught my scent, he looks at me like he can hardly believe what he's seeing.

"Now I know I'm hallucinating," he mumbles. "Damn moon fever."

I hurry over to him. His brow is slick with sweat. So is his muscular chest. Padding wraps around his wrists, keeping the silver cuffs from burning his skin, while the length of chain is snaked around him.

Cinder block dust is in a pile beneath the points where the chains are screwed into the wall. They've held tight, though not for a lack of trying.

When the worst of the fever hits him, he must put everything he has into breaking free of the chain and going to his mate.

Dropping to my knees, I lay the back of my hand against his forehead. Burning up, just like I thought.

Because I'm not his mate, I expected him to jerk away from my touch. He doesn't. He leans in, gasping as if he's drowning in the ocean and he's just sighted land.

Just sighted his salvation.

"Trish..." he whispers.

"That's right. It's me. No hallucination, either."

"Why? It's not safe... you shouldn't be here."

I ruffle his sweat-soaked hair. "There's nowhere safer for me in all of the world than right beside you, Duke."

"No. You don't know... not tonight. Not the Luna..." His eyes go from gold to hazel, then back to gold again. "I can't fight her. I'd fight anything for you, baby, but not the Luna."

My heart skips a beat when he calls me 'baby'. He's never done that before. I've been Trish, and I've been Patricia, but... I want to be Duke's 'baby'.

That seals it. I don't know what tomorrow will bring. Tonight, though, I'm going to be his 'baby'.

"You don't have to fight anything," I tell him. "Not tonight. But... you've got moon fever, don't you?"

"It's so hot," he murmurs. "Why is it so hot?"

He isn't wrong. I was burning up myself already, but once I got my first eye full of a near-naked Duke? I'm about to combust.

"It is hot," I agree. "I'm hot, too. You... you wouldn't mind if I took my dress off, would you?"

His eyes flash. "Don't tease the beast, baby. Please... you don't know what you're doing."

I know exactly what I'm doing. "It's the moon fever," I explain. "I'm hurting, Duke. I'm burning up. You said you'd take care of me—"

He snaps his teeth. They're not fangs. The silver keeps his wolf contained, so they're not fangs. That doesn't change the meaning of the gesture. "I will *always* take care of you."

"You asked me why I'm here. It's because I know you will. And, right now, what I need is something only you can give me."

"Oh?" He blinks rapidly, as if trying to focus. As if trying to understand that I'm really here. "What's that?"

I move into him. Then, before I can think better of what I'm about to do, I grab the erection straining against his worn jeans. "This."

He could've told me to back off. He could've shoved me away. He could've even hoisted his hips, pressing his hard-on against my palm.

He doesn't do any of that.

Instead, he crosses his arms behind me. Duke's not

quite touching me—he's holding his arms out so that the chains can't reach me—but I'm all but trapped in his arms.

"I've got you," he rumbles.

"No," I say, reaching down to unbutton his jeans. "I've got you."

Duke goes immovable still the second it registers what exactly I've done. I maneuvered myself within his arms, and now I've got one button done. Two buttons done. With a quick tug, his zipper is down and his cock...

Oh, Luna.

He's a big male. I already knew that. Of course his dick would be proportional to his height and his bulk. However, when I see the monstrous crown winking up at me, followed by the length that springs out now that his jeans aren't confining him... yeah. Only my unswerving resolve and absolute belief that this male will never hurt me

"Whoa." That's all I can say. Except for, maybe, "Luna, Duke. This is going to feel amazing inside of me. I mean, if you're willing."

A rumble rises up from his chest. "Trish Danvers is offering to let me stick my cock inside of her. I'd have to be a fucking idiot to refuse." His laugh is low and has my stomach clenching.

Or maybe that's my empty pussy.

"Just further prove this is a fever-filled dream. No way this is real life."

I run my finger around the head of his cock. When he sucks in a breath, I smile up at him. "Tell me. That feel real?"

"That feels like I'm about to come in my jeans."

"Uh uh." I waggle my finger at him. He groans at the loss. "No coming until I've got you where I want you. Deal?"

"I should be the bigger male—" he begins.

"Believe me. You are."

His eyes glimmer. "I should tell you to go. Even if you're just a dream, I shouldn't take advantage of you—"

I jab him in the chest. "I think I'm the one taking advantage of you."

"You're not. Because I want this. I want *you*. So I'm not going to tell you to go again. You're here, you're hot, and I've never felt anything better on my cock than your dainty hand. You need me to take care of you. I'll do that and more. You got a deal."

I chuckle, pleased that this seduction went a whole lot easier than I expected. "You could've just said 'yes'. But I guess I can accept that, too."

In answer, he snaps his teeth again.

"One thing, though. Don't bite me." I don't know why I say that. It's not like he can—not with his fangs, at least.

Then again, maybe I *do* know. Every young she-wolf is warned never to let their partner mark them on the full moon unless they want a mate bond. That's how the Luna Ceremony is performed, after all. And while I'm willing to take Duke away from his intended for just one night, I refuse to steal another female's happily-ever-after.

"If that's what you want, I vow to the Luna I won't. I won't hurt you at all, baby. If this is what you want, I'll make you feel good."

In answer, I glance at his arm. "Drop them."

He does.

Climbing out of his embrace, I quickly reach for the hem of my dress, discarding it in one frantic motion. I toss it away, knowing I'll need it to cover me up in the morning, but for now...

"Get on your knees, Duke." As soon as he does, I point at the ground. "Sit back on your heels."

My need cranks up to eleven when I see how submissive this normally dominant male is.

Whether he realizes it or not, I've just gotten him in the perfect position for me to mount him. I figure, when this is all said and done, he can justify saying 'yes' to mating me because I did the actual work. Especially since he's chained to the wall, there isn't much of a choice unless I want to risk getting burned. Even if I did, no way will Duke allow it.

No. The only way to get this started is for me to climb up on him.

Just in case, I check with him as soon as it's obvious what my intentions are. Looping one arm around his neck, I straddle his thighs, spreading my legs so that his bobbing cock is prodding my inner thigh.

"Is this alright?" I ask. "Do you mind if we do it like this?"

"You can do whatever you want to me. As far as I'm concerned, I'm still hallucinating. This can't be real."

It is, Duke. It is.

I grip his cock so that I can aim. It's a little unnerving when I can't close my fist around his girth, and if it wasn't for the moon fever spurring me to do this, I think I would've wimped out entirely.

The second I work his head inside of my pussy, I almost do.

His eyes, a glazed-over gold, narrow on me when I stiffen. "Trish, baby... you don't have to do this. If the moon fever's got its claws in you, I can make you feel good without mating. I can lick you and touch you until you're ready to take this step."

I'm ready now. I have to be. This is my only chance.

I push, and the head goes in. So does the first inch or two of his cock.

"No. I want this. It's just... oh." I knew there would be a little discomfort, a little resistance, but the pressure... it's a lot. My body is primed to mate, both me and my wolf willing. That doesn't change the reality that Duke is huge and I'm not. It'll fit... I just need a second. "I'm okay." Leaning forward a bit, I don't feel as stuffed as before. I wiggle, and the slight panic ebbs as I sink further down on him. "It's not as easy as I thought, but I'm okay."

He brushes my hair out of my face. Duke's watching me closely now, and there must be something he notices in the grimace I'm trying to hide that has his whole body going taut.

"Trish, baby... is this your first time?"

I don't answer him. I'm afraid if I tell him that it is, he'll stop me. Of course, if he changes his mind, I would climb off of him—but I've come this far. My wolf is telling me that is right. This moment with Duke, with the Luna out and the moon fever raging through me... it's *right*.

I just need him to agree with me.

In my feverish brain, I decide that, if I can get seated, then start the actual mating, I'll distract Duke from his question. Why I thought so, when Duke's proven to be immovably stubborn in his own way, I have no idea, but that's my plan.

I take another inch of his impressive cock inside of me before he shakes out the length of chain, getting it as far away as possible from me before he lays his hands on my hips. He doesn't squeeze, but his gentle grip is enough to keep me exactly where I am. Half-pinned on his length with no relief in sight, he tilts his head back so that he's staring at my eyes instead of my bare breasts.

"Trish... am I the first male you've ever mated?"

It's a ragged whisper, his wolf finding his way out in his tone. There's possessiveness there, undeniable need, too, and something I can't quite put my claws on.

Whatever it is, it's obvious that he won't let either of us move a centimeter until I answer his question.

My hands are still on his shoulders. Taking care not to prick him with the claws I can't retract, I knead the tense muscles. "Does it matter?"

Duke shudders. "It shouldn't. Luna knows it shouldn't. But I'd be a fucking liar if I said that it doesn't make me feel some kind of way that you chose me for your first. I'll take you any way I can have you, Trish, but I've gotta know. If it's your first time, I gotta do right by you. I gotta be careful."

That's exactly what I don't want.

I don't know what comes over me. It's like I have some desire to show Duke that, sure, he might've seen me at my lowest, but I'm made of stronger stuff than that. That doesn't excuse the fact that, my wolf in control, I lash out with my hand.

My claws rip down his throat, leaving four thin bloody tracks in its wake.

"You slashed me," he says in awe.

I swallow the apology that rises up. If he looked angry, I might've, but he looks... amazed? "Hey. It got your attention, didn't it?"

"It most certainly did."

His blood is trickling down his throat. I have this urge to lick it up, so I do.

"Oh, Luna." I don't know what I did, but his grip on my waist loosens. Wiggling just enough, I sink a little further down. He groans. "Trish, you're fucking killing me."

"I'm not," I promise. "I'm just fucking you. Listen... I... I don't want careful. I know you're gentle, but I don't want that tonight, either. I just want you. Is that okay?"

"You want me? Then take me."

He jerks up. A sharp pain, almost like a pinch has me gasping, but even before he's checking to make sure I'm okay, it's fading away into something blissful. Duke's seated himself entirely inside of me, and I've never felt more whole in my life.

"Yes," I breathe out. "Yes... this is exactly what I wanted."

"How is it? Are you okay?" he asks again. "Did I hurt you?"

"No. But if you don't do that again, I'm going to hurt you some more."

He chuckles. It's a strained sound, yet somehow relieved. "Mark me all you want. I won't bite you... I swore I wouldn't... but my body. It's yours, Trish. Use it however you want."

That's all I needed to hear.

I move slowly at first, then pick up the pace when the pressure becomes a consuming pleasure. He reaches parts inside of me that I didn't think could be touched, all without doing a damn thing but perching on the floor, hands behind him as I hold on tight and ride.

After a minute or so, I start to whimper. I need something else. I... I don't know *what* exactly, just that I'm racing toward a pinnacle that won't be reached without a little help. I've come before. In the quiet of my bedroom, rubbing myself to thoughts of what it would be like with a strong male... I've come. Always a tiny pop of pleasure, then a relaxation that almost has me humming before I fell asleep.

This is so much more. The friction of my pussy slamming down on him is a feeling I've never known before, my clit bumping with every pass. I reach between us, rubbing it frantically. That helps, but not enough.

And that's when Duke lifts his hand—claws sheathed—and grabs my boob. He tugs the nipple, flicking it with his blunt fingertip, always angling his hand so that the chains are away from us. My whimpers become pants, and my pants become a shout of triumph when he takes my nipple between his teeth, laving it with his tongue, just as I begin to climax.

He waits until I'm finally coming down from it before he trades sucking on my tit for nuzzling it, a hoarse shout vibrating against my clammy chest as he follows after me with his own orgasm.

I grab his head, clinging to him, as he comes inside of me. I'm not sure if I'm suffocating him, keeping his face pressed against my books, but he doesn't push away. In fact, he shoves himself closer, slamming into me so that we're completely one.

Finally, he finishes, and he starts to let his head fall back on his shoulder. Since I don't want him to pass out on me now, I tug his hair, then allow him to breathe again.

"Is that it?" It feels like I've taken the tiniest edge off of my lust, but Duke just came inside of me. That doesn't mean anything since we're bonded mates—I've only heard of one incomplete mating that led to a pup, and she ended up being the second female alpha in our history so I'm not worried about it happening to me—except he finished. "Are we done?"

Duke's husky chuckle sends a shiver down my spine. With a quick twist of his hips, I realize something. He's still hard. I feel fuller than before, almost as if something is keeping us connected.

"I never thought I'd have you like this," he rumbles, his hips jerking upward, ripping a moan from my throat at just how fucking *amazing* that felt. "Now that I do, I'm not going to let you get away that easily. Why? Do you want to go?"

There's something in his throaty tone. I know without a doubt that, if I told him I did, he'd found a way to separate us, then take care of his erection on his own, chains and all. I come first. He made sure I was with him all the way even though *I* seduced *him*. Even after he spent inside of me and obviously wants to again, that hasn't changed.

Ghosting my fingers over the first marks I left on his throat, I wrap my other arm around the back of his neck, tugging his mouth up to mine.

I kiss Duke with all of the pent-up need and passion I've been denying for months now, then nip his bottom lip with my fangs as soon as I'm forced to pull away. I've gone light-headed from lack of breath, but the heavy-lidded gaze he gives me, blood beading on the lushest part of his lip, has me eager to see what else my male can teach me.

"I want you to fuck me, Duke," I tell him boldly. Because that's what this is. It's mating, yes, and casual sex between two friends. But nothing about his Luna-given body is all that casual, and the rawness of the act is nothing less than fucking. "Until I don't know who I am or what I've done, I want you to take care of me like you said you always would."

"Like I always will," he vows darkly.

I gasp at how fierce he sounds, giving him the perfect opportunity to kiss me now.

I taste his blood and nearly come again at how sweet it is against my tongue. Lapping at his lip, I start to grind my pussy against his groin.

He rips his lips away from mine, eyes a blazing gold as he drops his palms to the concrete, lifting me off the ground with nothing more than the strength of his pelvis as he thrusts impossibly deeper inside of me.

"Ah, Trish, baby. You said you wanted me to take care of you. To fuck you. Stick your claws in me and hold on tight, because, tonight, your male is going to do all that and more."

Your male...

I know he doesn't mean it. He can't. He's meant for someone else. Then again, maybe he's right. Tonight he is my male, isn't he?

And when he uses his strength to shift our positions, spreading me out on the cool basement floor while pounding away inside of me, I don't know what's fucking hotter about this side of Duke I've discovered.

The way he finally treats me like a she-wolf instead of a pack princess that needs to be coddled—or the way the silver chains rattle as he fucks me again.

HOURS LATER, WHEN THE MOON FINALLY BEGINS TO SET, trading places with the sun in the sky, I climb off of Duke for the last time. He's impressively strong, but the silver will drain even the most powerful supe. His cock was willing, though the rest of him was fading, so that latest round ended with me the way we began: with me perched on his thick thighs, sinking down on his cock over and over again while he buried his face between my breasts.

I still have some energy. Just enough to separate our slick bodies and flop down near him, but it's gotta be more than Duke has.

And I believe that until I see his cock is still semi-hard, and his eyes are glazed with both exhaustion and lust as he watches every single move I make.

"Don't tell me you're leaving so soon?"

His voice is a rasp. Probably from all of the times he shouted as he came, or the ragged ways he called my name as I learned every inch of his sculpted body. I left my mark on his shoulders and his throat, and some on his thighs from when I reversed my position and rode him wildly while he kneaded away at my breasts. Tapping into my wolf since the silver kept Duke from using his, I shredded his jeans off of him and kind of, sort of clawed him up, too.

He didn't mind. In fact, he moaned any time his blood perfumed his air. He cut off my first apology with a kiss so deep, I realized that he... he *really* didn't mind. Duke actually started to piston his hips, reaching up to meet me on every bounce even though the concrete floor of the basement had to have chafed his poor ass raw.

He'd be completely healed by morning. The twinges in my pussy, battered ever so deliciously by his cock, would be a memory I treasured and nothing more. That's the best thing about being a shifter. No matter how wild we get, there's no injury during a mating we can't heal.

The aches are already fading as the moon loses some of her hold on me. It won't be morning for a few hours more, and there might be time for another mating after we rest for a while.

So, no. I'm not going anywhere.

He grins when I tell him so, leaning forward to nuzzle my nearest boob. I scoot closer so that I'm within his reach, and to the sounds of his content rumbling, I fall asleep.

I don't know how long he stays away while I slumber, curled at his side. His body warmth made it so that I didn't miss the dress I wore when I came to see him. In fact, sticky with sweat and overheated myself, I could've used a fan down here.

Figuring that's the last lingering effects of moon fever, I decide to see if I can wake Duke up. My internal clock says it's early, but not so early that I can't take the chance to mate him one more time before I leave and have to put the most memorable night behind me.

He has an intended. A mate that he hasn't claimed yet. Just because he was available for me to fuck his brains out this full moon doesn't mean that he will be next month.

I have to take him while I can.

Rising up on my knees, I think about grabbing his

cock to wake him up. The monster between his legs is already hard again so I'm pretty sure he'll welcome the interruption to his well-earned rest. Maybe if he *was* my mate, I would... but even I think that's probably too familiar for what we are.

So, instead, I reach out my finger, ready to nudge his shoulder.

I never make it.

Before I do, I reluctantly pull my gaze from his dick, glancing up at his slumbering face. That's when I see it. For a heartbeat, one terrible moment in time, I wait for it to be a mistake. To be my imagination.

It isn't.

Last night, when I begged him to take care of me, his throat was a thick column of unbroken skin.

That was last night.

This morning? It's not unbroken any longer.

It's *scarred*.

And I'm the one who gave him the marks he now has permanently etched on the side of his neck.

CHAPTER 8
RIVER RUN

I've never been so Luna-damned grateful that Duke can sleep like the dead before now. He was so careful not to let the silver chains brush me, even after we collapsed in a heap of sweaty, sated limbs together, he angled his gorgeous body away so that I didn't accidentally get burned.

That makes it easy for me to untangle myself from him. And I have to. Someone will be coming by to let Duke out of the chains soon, whether it's Bobby or Grant or any of the other pack council members, and I have to be long gone before they do.

I'm glad I came to him. I'm glad that Duke and I mated. We went into the act knowing that it was just sex. Just a way to work out the need that was riding us both. If he said 'yes' to me, it didn't matter that his erection was meant for anyone else. In that moment, it was mine.

Duke was mine.

But I wasn't supposed to *mark* him.

I... can't believe I did that.

Standing over him, I stare at the thin white lines that travel the length of his throat, horror building. No denying that the bloody marks from last night have faded to a stark scar. I don't understand. They should be gone. Like, I know that I was out of my head with lust when I clawed him, but *they should be gone*. There's no good reason why the cuts have turned into a set of scars instead of healing. Enough time has passed that, with his regenerative properties, Duke should have healed completely while we curled up against each other, sleeping off the rest of the fever.

Should be gone.

Should have healed.

Isn't.

Am I seeing things? I know I'm not, but I have to double-check anyway. It just doesn't make any sense. Shifters don't scar. Unless we use a silver compound to create a shifter tattoo, or we purposely keep the mark, it'll disappear shortly after we've been injured. For those lines to linger on his thick throat, Duke must have wanted them to stay.

Why? I... I have no idea. I thought I made it very clear last night that this was just another way for him to take care of me. I needed him, and once he under-stood how desperate I was, he was more than willing to give me what I needed. And, sure, I told him he could do whatever he wanted to me as long as he didn't mark me, I made no promises.

But that was because I was sure that he'd erase any marks I gave him. He'd have to. If he had a mate out there that he was drawn to but, for some reason, couldn't have, then he wouldn't want to wear evidence of our mating on his skin... right?

That's what I thought. That's what I expected.

So why are they still there? Because they are. They totally are. Four thin lines run jagged down the side of his neck. Duke is a big guy. A strong male. Anyone who sees those scars will know exactly how he got them. It wasn't a challenge that left him marked, it was a female.

It was me.

Worse, I marked a male with an *intended* mate.

That's the reality come crashing down on me as I crawl away from him. Last night, I was so desperate, I didn't care that the chains were evidence that he was meant for someone else. I might have decided that Duke was the perfect male to mate the first time, but that just meant we were two adults sharing one night together. He was suffering from the moon fever as much as I was, so it couldn't be helped. He wasn't a bonded male, and until I saw those chains, I didn't think he had a mate of his own in mind.

He agreed, I tell myself. This isn't Gem and Ryker all over again. He could've said no... but would I have pushed it if he did? I want to believe that I wouldn't have, but when you take a look at my track record... I'm not so sure I would have.

It doesn't matter that I was responding to the Luna's pull on me. Every shifter knows that moon fever is real. For unmated shifters, it's a nuisance more than anything. I've known packmates who get through it by exploring each others' bodies, and those like me who just grin and bear it. It's no picnic, I promise you, but it was manageable.

Last night was... not. I always heard that the needs get harder and harder to resist as soon as there's some kind of bond between two shifters. Whether it was fated or chosen, it didn't matter. He had a bond, I propositioned him anyway, and when he said 'yes', what did I do? I clawed him—

—but he kept them.

He called himself my male.

It was only supposed to be for one night... I wasn't supposed to steal someone else's forever!

Last night, I didn't really care about tomorrow— but now it's tomorrow, and that was precisely the attitude that got me banished from Accalia last summer. I committed the most cardinal sin among our kind: I tried to worm my way between a pair of fated mates. Ryker rejected Gem because of me, and he spent the next twelve full moons in a pair of chains because of me.

I found Duke in chains, suffering the madness that goes along with the moon fever. I knew what that meant. From the moment I saw him like that, it was obvious that he was restraining himself to keep from going after his female.

And what did I do? I went after *him.*

He thought I was a hallucination. He knew I was Trish, but he didn't think I was real.

Well, when he wakes up and discovers that I'm gone, maybe he'll think it really was a dream.

Too bad the scars on his neck will tell a totally different story...

RIVER RUN IS THE NEAREST SHIFTER TERRITORY TO Accalia.

I always knew that. Growing up, they weren't our allies per se, but we could rely on them in a pinch. That's why, when I got banished from Accalia, the obvious thing to do was hope Kendall Rivers—the Alpha of River Run—would take me in.

I'm not made to be a lone wolf. I'm a pack shifter through and through, and if I couldn't stay on the mountains, I at least wanted to be around my own kind.

Kendall was willing. I'll give him that much. But the price to gain entrance to his pack was one I couldn't pay, even after being banished. I had to forsake my family, forsake my friends, and give up any chance of ever returning home. If I didn't, if I betrayed River Run after pledging my loyalty to Kendall, he told me he would take it as a challenge and hunt me down.

I respected him being upfront with my choice. Knowing I could never give up hope on returning home, I had to decline, and I was scavenging on the land between his territory and Ryker's when Gem's vamp friend, Aleksander, found me and told me what to do and say to earn my ticket back to the Mountainside Pack.

Did I know he was using me? Of course. After Shane, I was beginning to be a pro at recognizing the signs when a male was manipulating me. He wanted Gem, he thought I still wanted Ryker, and he thought putting me back on the mountains would get us both what we wanted.

He was wrong. I gave up on Ryker even before I was banished, and all I wanted to do was rejoin my pack and make amends for my behavior. And I did—until Barrow slipped under my guard and tricked me...

When I left Ryker's old cabin earlier this morning, I didn't go home. Duke would know to look for me there, and I needed some time to figure out how I was going to deal with my reckless behavior. There was no taking back what I did. I marked him under the full moon, and I only hoped the fact that he didn't mark me means that I can salvage our friendship.

His mate might never forgive me for leaving those scars on his throat. I still can't understand why he wouldn't heal him, though I guess the moon does strange things to us all. Before yesterday morning, I didn't think I'd jump a chained-up Duke Conlon, either, so here we are.

On my run out, I realized that there probably wasn't anywhere in Accalia I could hide from him. He'd find me, if only to apologize, and that... I didn't like the idea of that, either.

So I kept on running.

I stayed in my skin for no other reason than my wolf was pissed at me. She didn't want to come out and aid in my escape, not when she thought I should've stayed behind with Duke. I can still run pretty quickly in bare feet, so I do, and before I know it, I'm edging up to the south side of River Run territory.

Because he's as anal and protective of an Alpha as Ryker, I'm not surprised to see Kendall pacing the lengths of the border as I approach.

I could avoid him. Technically, I haven't breached his territory yet. I was just heading for a place that I knew well enough that allowed me to put some distance between me and my mistakes. No surprise, then, that I took the same path I did right after I was banished.

I could avoid him. I don't.

I jog over to where he's standing, making sure to keep a good amount of distance between us as I wave over at the Alpha.

"Hey, Trish. Long time, no see."

"You, too, Kendall. Looking good."

"Always." That's an Alpha for you. I might be vain, but there's no shifter vainer than an alpha wolf. "What are you doing around here?"

If it was anyone else, I might have gotten out of having to answer that. I'm too ashamed to admit the truth, but this is Kendall Rivers. He's an Alpha whose only loyalty is to his people. And while I tried to petition to join his pack last year when I was banished, he knew all along that *my* loyalty was to Mountainside. If he thinks I present any threat to his people, he's not going to let me walk away without telling him why I'm here.

He sniffs. Before I can say a word, he nods. "Look at that. I guess congratulations are in order."

"Congratulations?"

Kendall nods. "On your new mate. You locked the big guy down. He used to be part of the traders, but he's Ryker's now. What's his name?" He snaps his finger. "Jack Conlon."

A lump lodges in my throat. I'm not sure if it's hearing Duke's old name—or just my reaction when Kendall's meaning finally hits home. I swallow roughly, then tell him, "He goes by Duke now. And he's not my mate."

Even if I wished he was.

With a snort, Kendall says, "Does he know that? His scent is all over. You don't have an alpha's nose, Trish. If you did, you'd know he left a musk that tells all other males to back the fuck off. You're taken."

What?

I shake my head. "No. It's not like that. It was the full moon. That's all."

He gives me a look of such disbelief, I begin to wonder if he's right. I know I smell like Duke and sex. But a warning? I don't get it.

He doesn't explain any further.

Instead, he says, "So why the run by? You thinking about petitioning to join River Run again? Because, I told you last time, I demand loyalty. You'd have to give up on Mountainside."

I could never do that.

With a half-grin of my own, I shake my head. "Thanks, but that's okay.

"That's fine." He jerks his chin. "So long as you stay on your side of the territorial line."

I make sure I do the rest of the time I spend away from Accalia. When the sun starts to set, the moon rising high again, I realize that I've probably been away too long. Following her glow as a beacon home, I chase the moon until I've slunk back onto Mountainside land.

For once, things go my way. No one stops me as I purposely make my way toward my cabin, ignoring my wolf's urging that I search out Duke. I'm in complete control tonight. No blaming moon fever when the Luna's pull on us both is far weaker tonight than yesterday. Tracking him down would be a mistake, and I tell my stubborn wolf that when she starts pacing around inside of me.

Or maybe she's only riled up because she can scent Duke all around my personal territory.

It's fresh. Even if I wanted to pretend that it was from any other night, I can't. Especially when I notice there's a foil-covered plate with a white square resting on top of it on my front porch.

He would've guessed I'd come in this way. He's gone—his scent at least an hour older—but he was here.

And he left me a note.

Crouching down, I pick it up. It's folded in four. My hands are trembling as I unfold it.

One line in a heavy block print stares up at me from the center:

We need to talk.

Folding the note up again, I crouch down and slip it under the plate.

I leave them both there. Before, I could fool myself and believe that he only left me food because he was treating me like a pup.

That all changed with the scars.

I know better now. Some way, somehow, a bond formed between us, one I neglected to see until it was too late. No denying that. Today, while I curled up beneath an oak, I finally listened to what my wolf was telling me. There's a shadow of a jagged bond inside of me, barely there but nowhere whole... and I know exactly who is on the other side. It's a bond, but it's twisted, broken just like me, and it's all my fault. I didn't mean to, but I marked him beneath the Luna. I took him from the female he was meant for, and I can only imagine how confused he must be right now. Especially since he would've woken up to me gone like that.

We need to talk...

He's right. But I can't.

Not now.

I just... I can't.

Locking the cabin door, I lean up against it with my back, staring up at my ceiling as I try to make sense of everything that happened since last night.

Too bad I can't do that, either.

Three days pass and I refuse to answer the door.

The first night, I caught a whiff of pine and I panicked. I'm not proud of it, but I bolted from my living room couch to my bedroom and slammed the door shut, putting some space between me and the front porch. Duke would know I was still inside my cabin, but I hoped he got the hint and backed off.

Based on the nightmares that haunted me each one of those nights, he did.

I can't sleep. I'm barely eating. My wolf is still angry at me, and I don't know what I'm supposed to do.

Then, to top it all off, four days after I slipped out of Duke's arms and left him on his own, Gemma Swann shows up at my cabin.

These days, she doesn't look like the pretty, porcelain doll she was when she first arrived in Accalia. Her blonde curls are usually slicked back in a long ponytail, her sundresses traded for a tank that shows off her muscular arms, and a pair of black jeans that match her alpha aura. Her honey-gold eyes are clever and shrewd, and the gleam brighter than the golden fang she wears on a chain nestled between her boobs when she glares over at me from her place on my front porch.

"Alpha?" I blink over at her. When I caught the dominant aura approaching my door, it never occurred to me to keep it closed. In the back of my mind, though, I guess I thought it would be Ryker out there because I'm shocked to discover the blonde alpha female standing on my porch. "What are you... I mean, can I help you?"

"Actually," Gem says, "I'm here to help you. Can I come in?"

She doesn't have to ask. She's the Alpha female. While I'm at the bottom of the pack's hierarchy with the rest of the deltas, she's at the tippy-top with Ryker. Even with her containing her dominant aura, I could never refuse.

"Of course. What's this about?"

"About you being Duke's fated mate."

CHAPTER 9
FOREVER

Gem takes advantage of my stunned silence to march right inside, kicking the door closed behind her as she says, "Figure you want privacy for this chat."

She isn't wrong.

It takes a second before I'm able to come out of it. "Duke's fated mate?" I echo. "I'm not his fated mate."

"Sure you are. Just because you don't feel the same way and you rejected the mate bond, that doesn't mean it didn't exist."

I don't... I don't understand. "I didn't reject him. I..." This is your female Alpha, Trish. She won't think any less of you, and to be honest, she probably already has an idea—if she doesn't already know. "I fucked him. How do you reject a mate after you fuck him?"

"Easy. By making it a point to tell him not to mark

you, then avoiding him while you stew away in your cabin, bringing down the rest of the pack."

Ouch. I'm not supposed to admit that I preferred Gem when she was a sweet and innocent-acting omega, but I was able to walk all over her back then. Not only is her dominance off the charts, but she's not holding back on me now.

What makes it worse is that... everything she just said is true. I did tell him not to bite me. I did mark him, though I never, ever expected he would take my claw marks and turn them into scars on his body on purpose. When I went to him on the night of the full moon, I'd hoped that maybe he might choose me. Even if only for that one time, I needed someone to choose *me*. I was willing to let him go to his intended when I was done—

—but, if what Gem is saying is true, *I*'m supposed to be his intended.

"I wasn't avoiding him," I lie. "I just... I had to figure out some stuff."

Gem snorts. "For future reference, babe? It's true that an alpha can sniff out a fibber. And you are a big honking liar. The only reason I came all the way down here to talk some sense is to you because no one else dared to bother precious Trish Danvers while she was moping. Not me. It's time everyone stopped protecting you."

"No one's protecting me!"

"And that's two. You want to lie to me again? Just because my mate let you back in the pack, it doesn't mean I forget what you put me through. I can forgive, Trish, but forgetting isn't something I'm too good at. Ryker made me promise I wouldn't challenge you or anything because he knows how much you still get under my skin. I want to prove to my mate that I'm better than that. Like it or not, we're both Mountainside. You and me... we're packmates. Fucking sisters, alright? So stop lying, and start listening."

I am. I heard every word of what Gem said—and, again, she isn't wrong.

"I'm sorry," I begin. What else can I say? "I'm so sorry."

"Forget it. We still got time to hash out our issues later. But that... that's me and you. I'm here about you and Duke."

It hurts to admit it, but... "There is no me and Duke."

"You're right about that. At least, if he goes through with this nonsense, there won't be."

I don't know what she means. "There never was to begin with."

"And who's fault is that? You were too busy mooning over *my* mate to notice when a big hunk of male arrived in Accalia and couldn't stop staring at you. You know why Duke asked Ryker's dad if he could stay? Because of you! He knew you were his mate, and when you didn't react to the bond the same way he did, he thought he already lost you to another male. And instead of leaving, that bonehead spent the next four years worshiping you from the distance—"

I can't stop myself from interrupting. "Me? He never said one word to me until he felt bad I got caught by *your* dad. Before that, I never noticed him. In fact, after you came along, he signed up to be your personal guard. He only started watching my back after."

To my surprise, Gem doesn't take my tone of voice as a challenge. She could, but she doesn't. In fact, she looks kind of impressed that I fired back. "He did. You can't blame Duke for that, though, any more than you can me changing his name. It's... it's an alpha thing. Just know that he didn't mean to pledge himself to me, and the moment he found out you were in danger, his feelings for you broke any hold I had on him. He loves you, Trish. So much that he set aside his own mate bond so that you'd be happy, no matter what. You rejected him four years ago when you barely noticed him, and you rejected him again this last Luna. And you're surprised he never told you that you were meant for him?"

"Meant for him? Really? Then where is he? He tried real hard to talk to me, right? But I haven't seen him in days!"

She raises her eyebrow. Scowling, fierce Gemma is gone. In a heartbeat, the suspiciously curious Alpha is in her place. "What? Are you telling me you don't know?"

If I did, I wouldn't have asked. I shake my head.

"Fucking males. I told him he could go talk to Elizabeth only *after* you agreed. Not to be all noble and go on his own."

Elizabeth. I know that name. She's the Luna-touched wolf who mated the head vampire in Muncie. The one who—

breaks mate bonds.

"Wait. I haven't sensed Duke in a while... are you telling me that he went to see her?"

Duke. The male who Gem just told me is my fated mate, who I marked during the night of the full moon, and who I've avoided ever since.

He's not my fated mate. He can't be. I would've known, right? Even if I didn't, he would've told me. For Gem to know everything she did—most of which happened before she even came to live with us—someone told her.

Why would he tell the female Alpha and not *me*?

That doesn't matter. None of that matters. Not if he really did what Gem said.

She nods. "He's there right now."

I dash for the door.

Smart Alpha. Fast, too. Gem beats me to it.

Blocking it with her body, she says, "You can't go."

"Move, Gem. I don't know what's going to happen

between Duke and me, but I can't let him do this. If we have a bond, I don't want him to throw it away without me getting a chance to explore what it means."

"He said you weren't happy. He thought, if he did this, you would be."

My laugh is hollow as I purposely meet her stare. "You should know better. I'm not the type of she-wolf who will ever be happy. Now move."

She puts her alpha voice into it. Her eyes glisten, a deeper shade of gold than I've ever seen hers turn. "You can't go, Patricia."

If her dominance hadn't made me give up my idiotic challenge, her use of my full name would have.

She gentles her tone. "We have an agreement. Mountainside shifters can't just walk into Muncie."

I did. After Aleksander Filan found me outside of Kendall's territory and brought me to meet the former head vamp so that I could get permission to enter Muncie and confront Gem... I walked around the Fang City without even a fang to shield me.

As though she's remembering that day last August when she found me pleading my case to Ryker, she shakes her head.

"Roman is gone," Gem reminds me. "Any pass he gave you died with him."

Aleksander is in charge now. The pretty vampire with the dreamy accent. "Ask your friend to let me in."

"I already called in the favor to get Duke in to see

Elizabeth. I can't burn another. I'm sorry, Trish. He said he would run this by you first. Elizabeth only needs one mate to want to sacrifice the bond, but I said he needed your permission, too."

Would I have given it? Selfish Trish Danvers?

No way in hell.

I already knew I wanted him. Am I in love with Duke? I... I think so. I never really allowed myself to think about that.

Do I want him to take away my chance to find out if this bond between us is real?

Nope.

"Gem—"

"You can't go," she says one more time, "but you can wait for his return. And you'll know, one way or another, if you still have a shot at your forever."

I guess that's as much as I deserve.

THERE HAVE BEEN TOO MANY INCIDENTS IN THE STRETCH of "no man's land" between Muncie and Accalia lately for me to feel comfortable waiting for Duke there. Instead, I find a spot about a hundred yards into the woods on shifter land, park my ass on a boulder, and wait for some sign that Duke is heading home.

It seems like hours, but it's probably only about one before his pine scent reaches me. All at once, the thoughts and questions and declarations I had ready to throw at him once I saw him again fly out of my head. Instead, when Duke comes within my line of vision, I do the most reckless thing ever.

I throw *myself* at him.

Good reflexes. My male—if he's still mine—has good reflexes. A split second before I reach him, he throws open his arms, welcoming me into his embrace with a tight squeeze as I try my very best to wrap myself around him like a fucking pretzel.

"I marked you." I sound as spoiled and as petulant as a four-year-old child who used marker to claim a toy as theirs. I don't care. "You're mine."

He folds me into his arms. "Oh, Trish. I always was."

"And it's not because of a bond," I rattle on. "One we had, one we don't, one we could've... When Gem told me before I never felt it... she was right. I didn't, but that's not your fault. It's mine."

His hand goes to my hair, stroking it reverentially. He probably has no idea what I'm talking about, what I'm doing here, why I've attached myself to him. I mean, I can sense his confusion—

I can sense his confusion.

It's not very strong, but it's there.

A bond.

Tears spring to my eyes. Before I know it, I'm a blubbering mess, smearing tears and—oh, Luna—snot on his shirt. All I get out is, "Don't leave me, I can be better," before dissolving into sobs.

I didn't cry the entire time I was in the Wolf District. Not one tear during banishment. But the relief I feel when I sense Duke on the other side of our twisted bond... forget being four. I'm a damn newborn.

"Shh... Trish, baby. It's okay."

I shake my head.

He continues to coo. "You didn't do anything wrong—"

Yes. I did. "I ignored the magnificent male standing in front of me for *four* years. I couldn't make it through one Luna once I realized how strong my feelings are for you."

Duke tightens his hold for a moment, taking in a sharp breath. When he exhales, he holds me at arms-length so that he can look down at my face. "Four years of full moons without you were worth it for the one we shared. But while I wanted you desperately, the moon fever didn't hit me until the last one. I wasn't sure how I would survive it and then... there you were, like an angel."

I give him a watery smile, tears still leaking down the corner of my eyes. I'm not sobbing anymore, but the relief is still overwhelming. "You said you were hallucinating."

"I thought I was. How else could a bumbling idiot like me lands the most gorgeous female in all of

Accalia? It had to be a dream. But if it was, then I'm dreaming again."

"Why? Because I'm holding you tightly? That's because I'm not letting you go. I said don't leave me. It's more than that. Stay with me, Duke. I need you to stay with me. And I need you to understand that I mean it. I was the idiot before. Not anymore."

Because he doesn't stay with me, I'm going with him. He can try to shake me off. I was willing to take on the female alpha to fight my way to him. I would've lost terribly, for sure, but Gem has a bit of a merciful streak. If she didn't put down her father after she challenged him and won, she'd probably just kick my ass and let me limp my way after Duke.

And I would. Bond or no bond, fate or not, this male is mine. If the Luna thinks so, that's just—pardon the expression—icing on the cupcake.

"I'm not going anywhere, baby." Ducking his chin, he presses a fierce kiss to my lips. "But that's not what I meant. I must be dreaming because I thought I heard you say you have feelings for me. Since they set off the fever and heat inside of you, they must be good ones."

Oh, Luna. Selfish Trish strikes again. Here I am, clinging to him like a barnacle, telling him he has to stay with me, listening to Duke tell me that he will, and I've let him think that I only want him around because of what happened on the full moon.

Yeah, right. Looking back, we both should've

known I was a goner when I sleep-shifted next to him. Nothing like falling asleep in your pajamas, then waking up naked next to your male to say: I want you. Even if my wolf wasn't giving me a nudge that I stubbornly resisted for too long, the cupcakes should've sealed the deal.

"They're the best," I promise. "Because I'm in love with you, Duke Conlon. And I dare any female to come between us."

Duke, my gentle giant, my silent shadow, the male I can't believe I didn't notice for so long... he throws back his head and lets out a howl that has my wolf jumping to her paws, my pussy growing wickedly damp in preparation for him to mount us.

That's a claiming howl and we both know it.

But first—

Slipping my hand between us, I tap him in the middle of his broad chest. "Well? Aren't you supposed to say something to me?"

Reaching around me, he places his hands beneath my butt. Without any effort at all, he lifts me up, urging me to wrap my legs around his waist. If we were naked, we could start mating right here, but luckily our clothes protect our modesty.

Even in a shifter pack, some things just aren't done —except on the night of the full moon, of course.

He kisses me again, almost as if he can't help himself, then buries his head in the crook of my shoulder. If he bit me now, it wouldn't matter—I could keep it as a scar, but it wouldn't become my mate mark until he fucked me again under another Luna—and I find that I'm becoming even hotter at the idea that I'll wear his marks the same way he wears mine.

As that thought rushes through my head, I dart out my tongue. I run the length of it over the thin white lines traveling down his throat. I made these marks. They're mine, just like Duke is.

And if I had any doubt that he feels the same way, they're immediately quashed when his deep voice begins to rumble against my skin, sending shivers skittering down my spine.

"I love you, Trish. I always have. I love the female you are, how you're loyal and determined and no one can tell you anything. From the moment I first saw you, I knew that there would never be anyone else. But you... you were looking at the Alpha while I was staring at you. And that was fine with me. I just wanted you to be happy. I'm only happy when you are."

Gem said that he went to break the bond because he didn't think I was happy. I threw in her face that I never was.

But when I cling to him, holding him tight, I realize something.

Duke makes me happy. Baking cupcakes makes me happy. Teasing Bobby, having sewing lessons with Audrey, taking odds on how much longer before Ryker and Gem start popping out pups... that makes me happy.

Hooking my hand around his thick neck, I pull back enough to meet his gaze again. "Look at me." He does. Duke doesn't even blink. "I'm happy. Fucking deliriously happy. But if you think you'll find some way out of this bond we have between us... like, say, asking a Luna-touched female to snap it? You'll see just how quickly you can piss a she-wolf off. You know your scars? I did that when I liked you. You don't want to see what happens when I don't."

I meant it as a tease. I'm so Luna-damned relieved he didn't throw away our shot at forever before I knew about it, I try to make light of the whole situation.

I should know better. That's not the kind of male Duke is—and I love him even more when he reveals another facet of his personality when his gleaming gold eyes turn almost defiant.

"I couldn't go through with it," he confesses. "I wanted to, for your sake, because I loved you too much to hold onto a bond that was making you miserable. But... in the end? I wanted you even more than that."

As if I didn't already know that. The moment I sensed him lumbering up the mountain in his skin instead of his fur, I knew... I just *knew* that his human side had taken the lead on the discussion with Elizabeth. His wolf wanted me, but it would release a mate who didn't recognize that they belonged together.

But his human side? It wouldn't—and I'm glad that it didn't.

I grin over at him. "Look at that. I guess we're both selfish, huh?"

And doesn't that make Duke Conlon the perfect mate for me?

EPILOGUE

A MONTH LATER

My head's cocked to the side, hair cascading over my shoulder as I sit at my kitchen table, waiting. I've got a loose curl wrapped around the pointer finger of my right hand. With the left, I'm running my fingertips over the thin white scars that pepper my collarbone.

That's not the only place I have marks. There's a noticeable bite on the side of my throat, a couple of slivers that trail the rounded curve of my boob from where Duke used one of his fangs. At my urging, he marked one of my butt cheeks, and that's not counting all of the tiny scars I have from when he gets too excited and his claws come out during mating.

I'm a shifter. If I wanted to, I could heal each and

every one of those injuries without leaving even the hint of a scar. But that's the thing. I don't want to. I spent my whole life being the empty-headed pretty girl with a bad attitude and a selfish streak. For so long, I believed the only thing I had going for me was my looks. I used to think I was perfect.

Ha.

A human might look at the white marks that cover me and wonder if I'm some kind of walking pincushion. A supe would wonder why my intended—because we're not fully bonded just yet—felt the need to scratch me up like that. But a she-wolf... she would know that I kept my marks because I treasure the physical proof that I'm wanted.

That I'm *loved*.

The first time we mated, I marked Duke. I know now that that was my wolf finding a way to send us both a message. Even if I was stubbornly oblivious to my feelings for him, my wolf, at least, recognized who he was to us. She was laying claim to him the only way she could.

Every time after that, I implored him to take his turn. My big mate was hesitant at first... until he woke up next to me the next morning and saw that the bite on my throat was still there. It nearly broke my heart when I realized he expected me to have healed it after he finished. As if. This male is mine, and he has been since I scratched his neck. It was only fair that I showed all of Accalia that I was his, too.

As if the rest of the pack didn't know. Audrey admitted that Grant was running a small pool, taking bets on how long it would take before Duke got up the nerve to tell me that we were mates. Seems as if *everyone* knew except for me, but because of his standing as one of Ryker's top enforcers, they didn't want to interfere in case I rejected him.

I can't even say that they're wrong. Duke knew for four years that I was his, but he watched as I did everything I could to get Ryker to choose me as his mate. He believed—like I did—that I was in love with the Alpha. That's why I never recognized the promise of a mate bond with Duke. He purposely shielded me from it so that I could shoot my shot with Ryker. And when he thought that I would be better off without him, he tried to leave.

Good thing I didn't let him go. I begged him to stay with me, and he has.

I wish I could say that, if he'd told me back then, everything would be different. I don't know if that's the case. That Trish might've done just what my pack-mates feared and thrown away a good male for one she could never have. No, Duke needed the Trish that went through hell and came out on the other side of it a better match for him.

Do I think I deserve him? Not even a little. He's too

good for me, though he begs to differ; that's why he tried to leave me, because he thought I'd be happy without him. Doesn't matter that he's wrong and I'm right. Selfish Trish marked him, she's mated him, and when he returns from tonight's council meeting, I'm going to make him my forever mate so that he can never try to leave me behind again.

Maybe then he'll finally get it through his thick skull that's the best thing that's ever happened to me...

I just... I can't imagine what's so important that Ryker needed to call his entire pack council to the den earlier this afternoon. Every single mature shifter in Accalia knows that tonight is the night of the full moon. Unmated shifters will be looking for some way to scratch the itch, bonded mates know better than to be separated when the Luna is at her peak, and an intended pair won't want to miss the one night of the month that their bond can be blessed and made whole.

The Wicked Wolf is no longer a threat to our pack. His Beta and the few sycophants he still maintained after the Western Pack disbanded are either dead or underground. The upheaval that happened in the Fang City on the edge of pack land when the old head vamp was murdered back in February has finally settled down.

For once, there's no hint of a Claws and Fangs war on the horizon. The vampires are keeping to their own business, and the shifter world seems to be calm again after the Alpha collective decided that the Luna-touched female with the gift to break bonds isn't a concern to the rest of us.

Any traitors in Accalia have been sussed out. Aidan Barrow—may the Luna curse his soul—was the last one, and though I know Audrey will never get over her brother's betrayal, it's been almost a year since Shane disrupted Ryker and Gem's Luna Ceremony. We have an Alpha couple that has brought stability back to the pack after the loss of our last one, and I finally have my future to look forward to.

Claws crossed.

As long as my future includes Duke, I can handle anything life throws at me. I proved it already, and though I had to rely on the strength of my mate to get this far, isn't that what a mate is for? A partner in life, someone who can hold me up when I'm too tired, too weak, too frightened to stand? Someone that I can be possessive over, and claim as mine, whether by the marks on his throat or how deeply my scent gets embedded in his skin.

Duke smells like something musky. Something woodsy. A hint of pine, of course, but also cinnamon. He smells like me.

Over the scent of the roast I have resting on top of my stove, sides prepared for a pre-mating dinner I made specifically for Duke, I search for some hint of him. Though he didn't know why the meeting was being called, either, he promised he'd be back before it got too late.

That was three hours ago, and I'm still waiting.

It's fine. I'm not worried that he's not coming back. I'm not afraid that he's realized what he's getting into, or that he's rejecting me. I know Duke now. In some ways, I've always known him. He'll be here.

He has to be.

Through the whisper of a bond that stretches between us, I sense him before I catch his scent. Jumping up, I make sure that I look okay. Because we both know exactly how tonight's going to end, I changed into one of my old shift dresses while I was waiting for him to come back to me. No bra, no panties, just a simple dress that will make it easier to get naked once I have my male where I want him.

Running my fingers through my curls, I pronounce myself as ready as I'm going to get. I have to remind myself that, while performing the Luna Ceremony is a much bigger affair for the Alpha couple, tonight is just for me and Duke. He loves me no matter what I look like, and even if I didn't do my hair and put on some make-up, he wouldn't care.

Still, it's definitely a boost to my confidence when I throw open the door for Duke a second before he reaches for the knob and my male's jaw drops when he gets a good look at me.

He breaks the trance after a moment, hustling me inside and closing the door behind us. The first thing he does after that is swing me up in his brawny arms, giving me one hell of a kiss 'hello' before setting me back on my bare feet.

I grin up at him. "Well, that's definitely a way to greet your female, isn't it?"

His cheeks turn a little ruddy as a hint of a blush colors them. "Sorry. I guess I just missed you more than I thought."

Wrapping my arms around his middle, giving Duke a greeting of my own, I tell him, "Never apologize for missing me. Especially since I probably missed you more." I lay my head against his chest, squeezing him in a hug, then ask, "What happened at the meeting? Is everything okay?"

Duke's hand is laying on the back of my head. With a gentle stroke, he runs his fingers through my styled curls. "You wouldn't believe me if I told you."

"I might. Try me."

His hand lands on the small of my back. It's so nice to stay in this embrace, but that doesn't mean I'm going to let him get out of answering my question. He's got me curious now, and though this position makes it obvious that he's as ready to mate as I am, I waited three hours for him. I can wait three minutes more to find out what was so important.

Tapping him on his back—and, okay, putting a

little pressure on his hard-on to catch his attention, I say, "Well?"

Duke sucked in a breath when I first made purposeful contact with his cock. Since he can tell that that's all the action he's going to get for now, he caves. Of course he does. This male will never me anything. "Okay. I'll tell you, but don't get mad."

My brow furrows. "Why would I get mad?"

"Because I spent the last hour listening to the other guys complain that their mates were going to go for their aching balls when we finally left. Turns out, the Alpha can be a bit of a prick. Gemma had to head into Muncie to take care of something, and since his mate wasn't going to be back until dark, he decided to distract himself by hosting a pack council meeting."

I shouldn't laugh. I was rubbing my pussy against the edge of my kitchen chair, I needed some kind of stimulation so badly, so Duke's right. I should be mad at Ryker for keeping my intended mate away from me for such a ridiculous reason. He had to wait to fuck his mate, so he made his right-hand wolves suffer, too.

I shouldn't laugh, but I can't help it. "Oh, Luna. I guess she made it back since you're here now?"

"Yup. As soon as he caught scent of her approaching Accalia, he kicked us all out." Duke finally joins me and chuckles, a husky sound that ruffles the top of my hair. "Good thing, too, because he was about to have a mutiny on his claws. Chains were the least of some of the suggestions the other guys were coming up with."

Yeah, right. I don't believe that for a second. Moon fever or not, Every shifter on the council is one hundred percent devoted to the Alpha. There might've been eight cases of blue balls going on in the den, but I don't doubt that the seven males on the council would cut off their own dicks before they challenged Ryker. He's earned their loyalty. Mine, too. If I had to spend my night crossing my legs tightly, trying to ignore my own need, I would've.

I'm just glad I don't have to.

With my hands pressed against his chest, I push far enough away from him that I can tilt my head back and meet his gaze without leaving the warm embrace of his arms. "You were that desperate to get to me?"

He presses a kiss to my lips. "Nothing will ever stop me from getting to you," he vows solemnly.

I believe him, too. Even when he was still part of Gem's guard, a trusted enforcer for the pack, he found his way to me in California. Following the side of a bond I never even knew existed, Duke tracked me to the cage they kept me in, then insisted on staying with me. He's been by my side ever since, and almost nine months from that moment, we're about to make it so that he'll never have to leave it again.

Luna willing, of course.

Standing up on my tippy-toes, I nip at his strong

jaw, then dance out of his hold. Not because I want to put any distance between us. The opposite, actually. There's just something I want to see first, and I start for the other side of the room.

He can't help himself. Like a puppy on a leash, Duke is inches behind me, trotting after me as I dash over to the window. I swallow my laugh of delight. When the only thing I've ever really wanted was to be the *one* to someone else, it still amazes me that—after all I've done—the Luna gave this male to me.

Or, I think as he settles his big paws on my hips, she will.

His warmth makes me shiver. His innate scent, swirling with notes of mine, has me almost whining with desire. My wolf is happy for me to take the lead in this, but she's growing impatient. She wants her mate, and she wants him now.

So do I, girl. So do I.

Duke bows his head, trailing his nose along the column of my throat. I'm not even a little surprised when he stops at the white bite mark that stands out against my tanned skin. Since the night he gave it to me, he seems drawn to it. Nibbling that spot, lapping at it with his tongue... it's all the proof he needs that I'm proud to be his.

After he presses an open-mouthed kiss to that very spot, he nuzzles his cheek against my hair while I angle my head up, glancing up at the night's sky.

There. Completely round and glowing brightly on Accalia down below, I see the moon in all her glory.

It's time. I knew it; as a shifter, I can sense the Luna all the way down to my bones. Still, with my entire forever on the line, it doesn't hurt to double-check.

"You see that?" I whisper. "Isn't she beautiful?"

"I'm looking at the most beautiful creature I've ever seen."

There's something about the way Duke says that. Almost reverential, as if he's worshiping our goddess, but with a promise that reminds me of the vows he made when we were locked together in Walker's cells. Laying my hands over his, I twist my head just enough to get a good look at his face.

He's not looking at the Luna. His hazel eyes gone a soft gold, my male is staring unblinkingly at me.

Oh.

Heat rushes to my face. I shouldn't be embarrassed. Since the night I seduced him during the last full moon, we've been together countless times. The half-bond that formed when I inadvertently marked him without asking for his—or the Luna's—blessing has only become stronger; tonight, it'll be whole. He's told me that he's loved me before. His actions over the last nine months made his feelings for me even clearer.

But the way he's looking at me right now... for the first time in my life, I really feel as if another soul *sees* me.

And, thank the Luna, it's Duke Conlon.

"Dinner's ready," I tell him. "I made pot roast, potatoes, and carrots. And some cupcakes for dessert."

His lips quirk in a small smile. "My favorites."

It's amazing how a tiny little grin can turn this male from handsome to heart-stopping, but it does. Ah, Luna... I'm not so sure I can wait until dinner.

I swallow. "I know. That's why I did it."

We're shifters. We can say 'I love you' with a meal, and that's what I tried to do today. The roast and sides aren't probably as good as the cupcakes will be, but I don't think Duke cares. It could be burnt and he'd gobble it gladly because I made it for him, and we both know it.

When he lets go of my waist, lifting his hands to my cheeks, angling my head so that he can take my mouth, I think he got the message.

By the time he pulls away, we're both out of breath. Not from the kiss, though. This is need, pure and simple, the Luna's power rushing through us. I'm panting, and Duke's expression has become inexplicably hungry.

I don't think it's for food. Just in case, I check.

"Did you want me to set the table, or—"

Before I can finish, Duke swoops me up in his arms. He has one hand wrapped around my back, the other cradling my butt, and he has me in a bridal carry as he starts to stalk away from the window, toward my bedroom door.

As he arrives at the entrance to the kitchen, he pauses.

"Will it keep?" rumbles Duke. He's asking me about the dinner I prepared.

I nod. "It might be a little cold, though, if we get... distracted."

His eyes brighten. It seems as if "distracting" me is exactly what he has in mind. "I don't mind if it gets cold. Besides, that's what they invented microwaves for. So, if you're okay—"

That's my male. Always worrying about what I think.

Luna, I love him.

I throw my arms around his neck. "Dinner can wait. I can't. It's time, Duke. Make me yours."

He crosses the threshold into my bedroom. "You always have been. Even when you didn't know it... you were always mine."

Maybe that's true. If Duke believes it, I'm not going to argue. But when he lays me down on my bed, stripping off my shift dress and his own clothes before settling himself between my legs, I realize something. It doesn't matter. The past doesn't matter. The way he loved me from afar without saying a word to me, and how much time I wasted chasing a fantasy when I had my forever right there... none of that matters.

All that matters is that, after tonight, all of my white scars will turn silvery, our bond will be whole, and Duke will be mine until the end of time.

I might not deserve him, but that's not going to stop me.

After all, it never has before.

AUTHOR'S NOTE

Thanks for reading *Stay With Me*!

When I first started this series, I only planned on writing Gem and Ryker's story. I wanted to give Janelle, Paul, and the Wicked Wolf their backstory, and that's how *Leave Janelle* came about. After introducing Elizabeth in *Forever Mates*, I just had to give Aleks his own story... and that led me to this novella. To end the series for now—because I still have an idea I'm playing around with—I wanted to show how two lost deltas... regular wolves with their own lives... could find love in their pack. You don't have to be an alpha or Luna-touched or the head vamp in a Fang City to be blessed with true love. Sometimes you can be a quiet newcomer or a broken she-wolf who didn't know what she really was missing, and the Luna will still bless you with the perfect mate.

AUTHOR'S NOTE

As I mentioned in the foreword, I do plan on returning to this world! *The Beta's Bride*—the second book in the **Stolen Mates** series—comes out in February, and I'm starting a vamp-centric series in the summer of 2023. I also plan on revising these characters in shorts from time to time (especially because I have something in mind for Jace, the current Mountainside Beta), but this is it. The main **Claws and Fangs** series is complete, and I thank all of your for coming along on the ride with me!

xoxo,
Sarah

PRE-ORDER NOW

THE BETA'S BRIDE

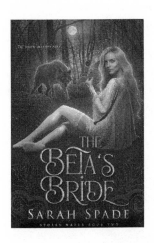

'Til death do they part...

Omegas are prized. I've always known that. Just like I grew up knowing that I would need a powerful mate to protect me.

I wasn't worried. I had Bishop—my overprotective alpha brother—to watch out for me, and then I fell in love with his best friend, Weston. A beta wolf, he was high enough in the pack that he would be a good match. And he loved me, too.

I couldn't choose anyone better.

Too bad it wasn't my choice.

Three years ago, I discovered that I was fated to be

the mate of the future Gravetail Alpha. Because of his rank, he couldn't claim me as his until after he was installed as Alpha, but it didn't matter. From the moment the Luna whispered my name to him, I was as good as promised to Rafael. With our alliance on the line, I had no choice.

And that meant I had to say goodbye to West.

Only... he didn't take it too well. Even after the Luna blessed him with a fated mate of his own, he rejected Quinn Malone, even while I counted down the months until I'd finally have to leave Hickory.

It's my duty. As an Omega, I don't have the luxury of choosing my own mate like Quinn did, and as much as it hurts, it's for the best when West finally becomes as cold and distant with me as he is with others.

I should've known better. After a five-year love affair, I should've known that meant he was up to something.

And when I wake up one morning with a ring on my finger and a mark on my shoulder, I find out exactly what it is.

Weston Reed has stolen me from our pack, and he won't let me go until I accept what he swears he's always known: that, fate or no fate, we're meant to be.

This Omega will be the Beta's bride—or no male's.

*The Beta's Bride is the second book in the Stolen Mates duet. After Quinn found her forever with Chase,

West decides it's now or never. He'll either have Helene for his mate, or... well, there is no *or*. And Helene? After a quick fright, she begins to accept that he might be right.

Out February 21, 2023

PRE-ORDER NOW

STOLEN BY THE SHADOWS

What if your imaginary friend was *real*?

Then again, Nox was never as imaginary as he was supposed to be, and while I thought of him as my friend, he watched over me because he knew we were meant to be more than that.

He knew that we were *fated*.

Me? I had no freaking clue, but that made sense. The last time I saw him I was twelve. He was the shadow monster that kept me safe. But, like all imaginary friends, he was just gone one day. And, as I grew up, I forgot all about Nox.

He never forgot about me.

Fifteen years later and he's still as much a protector as he always was. When I'm stalked by an ex who just can't accept that we're over, Connor isn't the only one who likes to hide in the shadows. Too bad for him that Nox *is* the shadows.

He's changed, though. My old imaginary friend is wrapped in golden chains, his shape unlike any he ever showed me before. He's big, and he's fierce, and he saves me from Connor only to take me for himself.

And I... I'm kind of okay with that.

---

* *Stolen by the Shadows* is the second book in the **Sombra Demons** series. It tells the story of Amy and Nox, the bonded couple introduced in *Mated to the Monster*.

Releasing October 25, 2022!

KEEP IN TOUCH

Stay tuned for what's coming up next! Sign up for my mailing list for news, promotions, upcoming releases, and more!

Sarah Spade's Stories

And make sure to check out my Facebook page for all release news:

http://facebook.com/sarahspadebooks

Sarah Spade is a pen name that I used specifically to write these holiday-based novellas (as well as a few books that will be coming out in the future). If you're interested in reading other books that I've written (romantic suspense, Greek mythology-based romance, shifters/vampires/witches romance, and fae romance), check out my primary author account here:

http://amazon.com/author/jessicalynch

ALSO BY SARAH SPADE

Holiday Hunk

Halloween Boo

This Christmas

Auld Lang Mine

I'm With Cupid

Getting Lucky

When Sparks Fly

Holiday Hunk: the Complete Series

Claws and Fangs

Leave Janelle

Never His Mate

Always Her Mate

Forever Mates

Hint of Her Blood

Taste of His Skin

Stay With Me

Sombra Demons

Mated to the Monster

Stolen by the Shadows

Stolen Mates

The Feral's Captive

Chase and the Chains

The Beta's Bride

Wolves of Winter Creek

(part of Kindle Vella)

Prey

Pack

Predator

Claws Clause

(written as Jessica Lynch)

Mates *free*

Hungry Like a Wolf

Of Mistletoe and Mating

No Way

Season of the Witch

Rogue

Sunglasses at Night

Ain't No Angel *free*

True Angel

Ghost of Jealousy

Night Angel

Broken Wings

Of Santa and Slaying

Lost Angel

Born to Run

Uptown Girl

Ordinance 7304: the Bond Laws (Claws Clause Collection #1)

Living on a Prayer (Claws Clause Collection #2)

Made in the USA
Columbia, SC
17 October 2022

69607001R00093